Victoria Taylor Murray

THE SHADOW OF HER SMILE

An Elite Publishing Company

Just My Best, Inc.

1746 Dailey Road
Wilmington, Ohio 45177

http://www.jmbpub.com

The Shadow of Her Smile

by Victoria Taylor Murray

Just My Best Book Publishing, is a subsidiary of
Just My Best Incorporated.

Manufactured in the United States of America

ISBN 1-932586-30-X

Victoria Taylor Murray, is a former Playboy Bunny/ model/entertainer turned mystery/romance writer of (11) novels (5) of which are published thus far), (150) poems & song lyrics, several news paper articles, several short stories, and (2) songs, "Lonely Hearts Cry" and "Since You've Been Gone," available on CD albums produced by HillTop Records in Hollywood California. For more information on this author visit her web site at http://www.authorsden.com/ victoriataylormurray

THE SHADOW OF HER SMILE

THE SHADOW OF HER SMILE – is a Romantic/Suspense taking center stage in New York City. An erotic tale of desire, disillusion, and obsession, connecting the lives of its (5) key characters — **Corbin Douglas**, P.I. Extraordinaire, a former N.Y.C Homicide Detective, now, the most sought after P.I. in the country. — N.Y.C. Homicide Detective, **Charlie Miller**, former partner in fighting crime with Corbin Douglas, also Corbin's best friend. — Billionaire Businessman, **Forrest Gray,** Corbin's newest client, and Forrest's attractive wife, **Jill Jefferies Gray**, a couple that gives new meaning to the phrase, "*till death do us part.*" Behind Jill's unbelievable beauty is a devious mind at work. — And, **Nikki Rourke**, Forrest Gray's current mistress, a young, exotic dancer, fearing for her life, Nikki goes into hiding after several of her closest friends are murdered. Afraid she will become the next victim on the killer's "hit list," Nikki vanishes into thin air.

Not knowing why his billionaire client had paid him so handsomely for such a "*cupcake assignment*" which was, to keep a watchful eye on Forrest Gray's young, red-haired mistress once her flight from France arrived at the J.F.K International, Corbin quickly realizes he has accepted a case that is more involved then meets the eye after the only beautiful, young, redhead on that flight was shot and killed the moment she stepped off the plane. Relieved to learn the young woman that had been killed wasn't his "Surveillance Subject," Corbin goes in search of the beautiful missing dancer racing against time trying to find her before the killer does. With more questions than answers and more suspects then he knows what to do with, will the famous P.I. get to the bottom of things in time to save the red haired beauty. *Someone wants his Surveillance Subject dead and in a big way. Whoever it is will stop at nothing to find her.*

CAPTIVATING & STEAMY

A great read and a different type of romance novel! Sizzling and erotic, (this old sailor discovered a page-turning mystery weaving through romance, steamy sex, and thrilling action! What more could a man of the sea want?) Taylor-Murray is catapulting upward in the romance-thriller genre. If you like Danielle Steel & Nora Roberts, you'll love Victoria Taylor Murray. Don't miss an opportunity to read her. Take a bow, Victoria. I, for one, look forward to seeing more of you. - Navy Captain, David E. Meadows, author of *The Sixth Fleet Series*, and *Joint Task Force Series*

THE EXCITEMENT WAS NONSTOP

"Reading *The Shadow of Her Smile* was like slurping a long, cold lemonade on a sultry, summer day—I couldn't devour it fast enough! The story started off with a bang, growing increasingly suspenseful as Victoria Taylor Murray drew me into her exciting plot with the ease that only the best writers can achieve. From Trump Tower to the Waldorf-Astoria Hotel to Little Italy to NYPD and a grandmother's run-down mansion, she painted a New York seldom seen by outsiders. I especially relished the historical vignettes of The Big Apple woven in at appropriate places in the story. Although many of the supporting characters were ultra-worldly—obviously shallow, greedy, and lustful—each one was unique and thoroughly fleshed-out. Through them, Murray captured the true essence of the city's diversity of cultures and life-styles. And the hero and heroine are to die for! The excitement was nonstop as handsome Corbin Douglas searched for beautiful, red-haired Nikki Rourke—a "woman in a photograph" with an unforgettable smile—overcoming death-defying, breath-stealing obstacles to help her. This well-written, fast-paced book has everything: believable characters, realistic dialogue, suspense, romance, and "original" humor. For example, when Corbin, a cop-turned-private-investigator, told his former partner, "I have a headache the size of Stephen King's Buick 8," I laughed out loud ... a welcome relief from the tension of the book's drama. I join this talented author's legions of fans in applauding her on penning another winner. My one regret is that I didn't discover her from her very first book." - Betty Dravis, author of *The Toonies Invade Silicon Valley*

SEXY MURDER MYSTERY

It's been awhile since Victoria Taylor Murray delivered a new book to her fans around the world. Her latest offering is a romantic suspense novel set against the backdrop of New York City. Fans will be happy to know she hasn't changed her style or flair for intrigue and sexy assignations. Organized crime, shady judges, beautiful people with love on their minds, and high-powered heroes join forces in this sexy murder mystery. Private Investigator Corbin Douglas is mildly curious when billionaire Forrest Gray hires him to keep a watchful eye on his young mistress. What Douglas expects to be an easy job rapidly escalates into a murder plot even he can't figure out. Douglas is a former Detective with NYPD and brings that experience to his P.I. business. He's very good at what he does, but is he good enough to keep Nikki Rourke alive? Nikki Rourke is a flame-haired, exotic dancer who performs at The Scarlet Ribbon. She's been alternately hiding and running for her life since several other dancers at The Scarlet Ribbon turned up dead. No one knows who killed them or why, but Nikki firmly believes she will be next. Her married lover fancies himself as quite the ladies' man. Were the murdered dancers one-time lovers of Forrest Gray's? Or were they killed for some other reason altogether? Either way, Nikki's taking no chances. She's gone underground and intends to stay there. Douglas is assigned to meet Nikki's flight from France as it lands at JFK airport. When a beautiful redhead is shot and killed while walking off the plane, he's relieved to learn it wasn't Nikki. But where is she? Who wants her dead? And will he find her before the killer ends her life? Each twist of plot introduces a new suspect and raises complicated questions for the harried P.I. as he searches for the frightened dancer. *The Shadow of Her Smile* is a tidy little thriller, complete with canny protagonists and vicious power players. It's sex and suspense, with New York City as the stage. - Laurel Johnson, Reviewer

MYSTERY, SUSPENSE AND TITILLATING ROMANCE

Be prepared to settle in when you pick this book up, because you will not want to put it down. Ms. Murray is well-known by her numerous fans for delivering fun reads, filled with mystery, suspense and titillating romance. Her masterful talent for characterization, innovative plot, and sensual romance once more prove beyond a doubt that Ms. Murray is destined to reach and become a mainstay on the *New York Times* Bestseller List. Highly recommended. -- Christy Tillery French, author of *Chasing Horses*

MORE THAN HE BARGAINED FOR

Former police officer, private investigator Corbin Douglas, has been hired to find red-haired model Nikki Rouke and to keep an eye on her while she is in New York. According to the information Corbin receives from wealthy Forrest Gray, Nikki is to be staying at the St. Regis hotel for two weeks. Rourke is not on the plane, a beautiful redhead is murdered in the JFK terminal and Douglas is soon embroiled in anything but the cupcake deal he had expected.

A murdered redhead in France and a third found in the room Nikki Rourke was to use, all add up to a whole lot more than Corbin Douglas had bargained for. Corbin's old partner, Charlie Miller, is drawn into the case. Each of the murdered women has a tie to Rourke, a tie to billionaire Forrest Gray and a tie to the owner of a new club, the Scarlet Ribbon. It is up to Charlie and Corbin to try to sort it all out before another redhead comes up dead.

A mob hit against a redhead, an auction at Sothebys, Nikki hides out in the old family estate, The Blue Gibson blues club, a chance meeting, wedding in the planning goes awry when the wedding planner comes up missing, Corbin suffers amnesia, Charlie issues a warning, helpful neighbors, a woman's body is fished out of the Hudson River, a secret wall safe, a break-in, the wedding of the century and a confession of murder all figure in the tale.

With the advent of The *Shadow of Her Smile,* writer Taylor-Murray has produced another in her exciting succession of complex narratives filled with energetic, engaging characters, thrill-a-minute story line rounded out with twists and turns in addition to varied and efficacious motivations. Hard-hitting dialogue filled with convincing passion set against an atmosphere overflowing with manipulation, mendacity and maneuvering, moves the narrative along at breakneck speed.

As we have come to expect from her previous works, Taylor-Murray's characters are robust, often precipitate and always filled with the human frailties, faults and imperfections common to us all. The reader is caught up in the narrative from the opening paragraphs as writer Taylor-Murray sets down a vivid picture of the New York City environs in which Corbin Douglas and Charlie Miller reside and work.

Reader interest is held fast in this roller-coaster ride teeming with homicide, disingenuousness, and cupidity, from opening lines to the last paragraphs as we face the faceless terror with Nikki, the harsh reality of death and deceit with Charlie Miller, and Corbin Douglas grappling with trying to remember who he is and what he is doing at the Rourke Estate. - Molly Martin, Reviewer

DEDICATION & ACKNOWLEDGEMENT PAGE

"The Shadow of Her Smile," is dedicated to my wonderful daughter, Michelle, my amazing son, Michael, and my beautiful daughter-in-law, Diane. *I love you my darlings, TWATC...*

I would also like to dedicate this book to my amazing family the *Taylors* too many to mention by name.

Others I'd like to acknowledge *for one personal reason or another...*

... Favorite Authors & Friends... Christy French, Norm Harris, David Meadows, Evelyn Horan, Sherry Russell, Lynn Barry, Beverly Scott, David Rehak, Janet Sue Terry, Gina Pounds, Nora Roberts, Danielle Steel, Dan Brown, John Sandford, Sandra Brown, Suzanne Brockmann, Elizabeth Lowell, and Janet Evanovich.

...Favorite TV & Movie Personalities (some of which) are also friends... David Letterman, Regis Philbin, John Savoy, Paula Abdul, Bruce Willis, and the *forever young,* Joan Collins.

Lastly, I'd like to acknowledge a few very special friends at Waltz Hitching Post in my hometown of Fort Wright Kentucky. One of the sweetest men in the world, Tom Cordosi, Paula Melton, Bill Melton, Terry Points, Melissa, Deb, Debbie, Linda, Sue, my main man, Tucker *aka* Dancer, Meghan, Alex, Stefy, Jennifer, Michelle, Jeff, Marty, Peg, Gary, Denise, Judy, Billie, Zeke, Glynn, James, Tom...all employees, too many to mention. I love you guys, you're the best!

As always I enjoy hearing from my many friends and fans. Email anytime! (vtm_inc@hotmail.com) or drop by my homepage http://www.authorsden.com/ victoriataylormurray.

COLORFUL CAST OF CHARACTERS

Corbin Douglas – Former New York City Homicide Detective turned P.I., now the most sought after private investigator in the country. Corbin's newest assignment, may just very well turn out to be his last as he goes in search of the missing young mistress to one of the wealthiest men in the world.

Charlie Miller – New York City Homicide Detective, former partner, and best friend to P.I. extraordinaire, Corbin Douglas. Charlie has his hands full as he tries to track down a deranged serial killer that is going around murdering beautiful, young, read-headed dancers who work for a new nightclub that just opened in his city.

Nikki Rourke – Beautiful, young mistress to one of the wealthiest men in the world. Also, a young woman that someone wants to see dead in a *"Big Way."* Will Corbin Douglas get to her before the killer does?

Forrest Gray – Billionaire Businessman and a man that fancies himself "Quite The Ladies Man."

Jill Jefferies Gray – Forrest Gray's wife of twelve years. Also a woman with a few secrets and skeletons she doesn't want her husband to find out about.

Jacqueline Collins – Former French Playmate/Exotic Dancer, turned nightclub owner of, The Scarlet Ribbon. Also, former lover to billionaire Forrest Gray.

Regina Prescott – P.I., Corbin Douglas, girlfriend and Regina is also a high-power criminal attorney.

Kramer Davenport – High-power, high-dollar criminal attorney.

Paul Cucchiara – Law partner with Kramer Davenport. Also, number one attorney to crime boss, Anthony Juliano.

Brill Miller – Works for the F.B.I., also, brother to homicide detective, Charlie Miller.

Gaberille Graves – Exotic Dancer who works at The Scarlet Ribbon.

Rachel ward – Exotic Dancer who works at The Scarlet Ribbon.

Cameilla Villano — Exotic Dancer and friend to Nikki Rourke.

Anthony Juliano – New York City "Crime Boss."

Sidney Cox – Jill Jefferies Gray's best friend. A young woman that gives new meaning to the word "best friend".

Clay Warner – Clay is the man that can hardly wait to marry Sidney Cox.

Tinker French – Tinker is a wedding coordinator that works for Gateau de Mers.

Franco Morissette – Franco is the gay dance instructor to all the dancers that work at The Scarlet Ribbon.

Dex – Franco's gay lover.

Judge Due – New York City "shady judge."

Asia Alexander Rourke – Exotic Dancer, Nikki Rourke's grandmother.

Bradley Rourke – Nikki's father.

Bradley Evans Rourk III – Nikki's grandfather.

Haley Theroux Callot – The aunt that raised Nikki.

Elizabeth Theroux Rourke – Nikki's mother.

Belle Rourke Byrd – Nikki's aunt.

Sybil Rourke Casey – Nikki's aunt.

Carmine "Blade" Asaro – Foot soldier for the "MOB."

Mr. Carvalho – Famous Fashion Designer.

Dillon – Head bartender at The Scarlet Ribbon.

Scottsdale – Forrest Gray's butler.

Atlantis and Katarina – Twin dancers who work at The Scarlet Ribbon.

Edward & Ellen Hollingsworth – Asia Rourke's neighbors.

Kyle Nelson – Handsome, young bartender that works at The Blue Gibson, Jazz Club. Kyle is also Nikki's former boyfriend.

Chapin Nelson – Head chauffeur for the Grays.

Bernice & Alfred Posten – Former maid and butler at Rourke manor.

Sela Lawson – Regina Prescott's secretary.

Marlee Fairbanks – Corbin Douglas's private secretary.

Ted Edward Stacy III – Former "*Sugar-Daddy*" to Jacqueline Collins.

Tommy Villano – Formerly worked for the "Juliano Crime Family," also, Camellia Villano's father.

Joey Mezzogiorno & Eddie "Styles" Costa – Undercover Agents for the F.B.I.

Sam Maloney – Sam works odd jobs for Corbin Douglas.

Morris Schiaffino – New York City's Police Chief.

Victoria Taylor Murray

THE SHADOW OF HER SMILE

Just My Best™

An Elite Publishing Company

CHAPTER *1*

NEW YORK—The city people love to hate. It's dirty. It's dangerous. The winters are unbearable. And the traffic is sheer madness. On the other hand, there's nowhere else on earth quite like it.

Where else can one appreciate choices from over seventeen thousand restaurants, one hundred dance clubs, one-hundred-fifty museums, four hundred art galleries, two-hundred-forty theaters, one-hundred institutions of higher learning, and thousands of shops and boutiques. It's truly a city that doesn't sleep. Ole' Blue Eyes said it best.

New York is serviced by three airports John F. Kennedy International fifteen miles from Manhattan in Queens the largest of the three airports that handles primarily International flights. La Guardia, also in Queens eight miles from Manhattan handles primarily domestic flights. And Newark, across the Hudson River in New Jersey handles both domestic and International flights. Kennedy is the most congested of the three airports. Newark the least.

New York private investigator Corbin Douglas, mumbled under his breath as he glanced at his watch, and then at the 'Sorry for the delay' sign. "My luck, I'm stuck battling it out in traffic with thousands of other poor bastards here at JFK."

JFK was currently in the midst of a $4.5 billion dollar redevelopment program.

"Jesus," the P.I. mumbled again, scratching his head at the thought, wondering how long the mess was going to go on in his city.

As the impatient private investigator sat bumper to bumper in traffic nervously tapping his fingers on the steering wheel of his newly restored Stingray, the image of his new surveillance subject's face flashed before his eyes. A face he knew right from the moment he first saw her photograph, it was a face that would be difficult, if not impossible, to forget.

Nikki Rourke, age twenty-six, emerald-green eyes, flaming red hair, a

1

body-to-die-for, and the most captivating smile he had ever seen. He slid her photograph out of the 8X10 manila envelope that also included her bio and a retainer check for one-hundred-thousand dollars.

His latest client was billionaire businessman Forrest Gray. And, Nikki Rourke was apparently the billionaire's mistress. Of course, Forrest Gray never came right out and said so, but the cloak and dagger request and the photograph of the subject in question rather matter-of-factly spoke for themselves.

Corbin continued to be lost in thought as he studied the photograph of the beautiful young redhead.

Corbin Douglas, Private Eye Extraordinaire, was New York City's most in demand private investigator. He was a former New York City homicide Detective, who had quit the police department three years earlier, and turned his P.I. business into one of the most successful private investigating businesses in the country.

Corbin's impatience continued to escalate. He glanced at his watch with a sigh of frustration.

"Mr. Douglas, I have a cupcake assignment that I know you won't want to turn down." His billionaire client had said to him two days earlier during their phone conversation. "I know its short notice, but for a hundred grand you shouldn't mind the inconvenience too much…"

A man shouting interrupted Corbin's thoughts. "Oh, my God! There's been a shooting inside the terminal."

Corbin instinctively shoved his car's gear into park and jumped out. "Hey, mister!" he shouted. "Which terminal?" He motioned to the excited man trying to attract his attention.

The man couldn't hear the P.I. over the commotion occurring nearby. "Shit!" Corbin spat, jumping back into his car. He pulled his Stingray into the only available parking slot within view, a handicap spot.

Corbin shrugged, knowing he would probably be ticketed for parking there. "Oh well," he groaned, making his way toward the closest terminal. His heart raced as his feet moved.

A uniformed police officer stopped Corbin when he tried to enter the building. "Damn it!" he cursed under his breath.

"I'm sorry, sir. No one's allowed to enter the terminal yet." The young cop's tone was nervous. He cleared his throat and then went on. "There was a shooting earlier. A woman…"

Corbin interrupted the cop. "A woman? Who was it?" he asked. He prayed it wasn't his new surveillance subject.

"I don't know who she was," the cop snipped with an attitude.

"What color was her hair? Can you at least tell me that much?" Corbin pleaded.

The cop looked at the P.I. as though he were insane. "Sir, please. I have no way of knowing that," he replied as he continued to stop people from entering the terminal as individual doors flew open, one after another.

Corbin raised his voice over the loud noise. "My name is Corbin Douglas. I'm a private…"

The cop interrupted. "I know who you are. You used to be a cop."

"Can I please slip through? It's very important."

The uniformed officer nodded his okay just to get rid of the P.I. and turned his attention back to the massive mob of people continuing to surround him.

Corbin wasted no time making his way to the baggage claim area, hoping Nikki Rourke hadn't yet been allowed to depart her flight just in from France.

He held his breath as he glanced around the busy area. The men on the scene from the coroner's office were about to remove the body of the young woman who had been shot a short time earlier.

"Oh my God!" he gasped, noticing the young woman had red hair. "Just a minute!" he called out. "Is she dead?" He reached out to stop the two men from placing the body of the dead woman inside a plastic zipper bag.

The two men nodded. "I'm afraid so." One of the men from the coroner's office replied. Corbin glanced down at the woman. He sighed in relief. The young woman wasn't his surveillance subject.

"Anyone you know, Corbin?"

He turned, as he recognized the voice of homicide Detective Charlie Miller of the New York City Police Department.

Corbin shook his head with a decisive no. "Who was she?" he asked, reaching inside his shirt pocket for a cigarette.

The police detective extended his arm to stop him. "Don't light that damn thing up in here, Corbin. You want to be cited?" He pulled the P.I. off to the side.

Corbin slid the cigarette back inside his shirt pocket.

"What brings you here?" The police detective asked.

"I'm working on a new assignment. I was supposed to tail…"

Charlie cut in. "Does this have something to do with redheads?"

"How did you guess?"

Charlie grinned.

"That obvious, huh?" Corbin mused.

"What's up?" the homicide detective inquired. "You're here tailing a redhead and a redhead barely steps off the plane, and its rest-in-peace Mrs. Colombo."

Corbin chuckled at the detective's sense of humor. "I don't know, Charlie. Maybe no connection at all. Has flight 648 arrived from France yet?" He glanced around the baggage claim area before checking his watch.

Charlie shook his head. "That's where Ms. Ward just flew in from."

"Shit!" Corbin complained, bringing his gaze back to the homicide detective. "Were there any other redheads on the flight?"

3

Charlie shook his head. "Nope, Ms. Ward was the only one."

Corbin looked thoughtful for a moment. "Wonder what happened to my redhead?"

The detective shrugged. "Maybe you should give your client a call."

"Looks that way, my friend." The P.I. said, turning his gaze back to the two coroners carting the dead woman away.

"Who's your client, Corbin?" the detective asked.

A grin curled the cocky P.I.'s lips. "I'm not at liberty to say," he replied.

Charlie shot his former colleague a look of irritation. "You want to give me a goddamn break?"

Corbin chuckled. "Come on, Charlie. You know how it goes. Some clients just don't..."

"Forget it!" the homicide detective said heatedly. "I'll remember that the next time you need another goddamn fav..."

"Don't have a cow, Charlie!" Corbin returned with a chuckle. "The guy I'm working for just paid me quite handsomely to..."

The homicide detective shook his head and stopped the P.I. from finishing. "Like I said Corbin, just forget it!" he snapped.

Corbin smiled, understanding his former partner's hot-temper. "Did Ms. Ward have a first name?" he asked.

The detective nodded. "Oh sure, most people do, Corbin. That is unless you're the pop star formerly known as Prince." He, paused, and then added, "If you don't want to share with me, then why in the hell should I share with you? You remember how it works. You scratch my back and I'll..."

Corbin stopped his former partner in fighting crime from talking when he made a cringing face. "Ah, no thanks Charlie. I'd rather not. Nothing personal, mind you." He laughed.

The detective shook his head. "Very goddamn funny, dickhead!" he barked, before shoving his hands into his trouser pockets and storming off.

Corbin chuckled as he too turned to leave the airport terminal. He rushed outside to find himself staring at his Stingray being carted away by a tow-truck. "No way," he complained, scratching his head. He raised his arm in an attempt to flag down a taxi.

New York's estimated population is a staggering 8 million made up of five boroughs, Manhattan, Brooklyn, Queens, the Bronx, and Staten Island all covering a little over 300 square miles.

The New York City Taxi and Limousine Commission licenses well over twelve-thousand taxis a year and the Nationalities of New York City's taxi drivers who speak little or no English usually hail from either Pakistan, India, or Bangladesh. Most of them have no idea where they are going most of the time.

"Swell," the P.I. whispered as he attempted to help the Bangladesh taxi driver with directions to his office in Midtown.

With the heavy influx of weekend travelers, heavy traffic, delays, detours, and the five-car pile-up on the freeway the private investigator was stuck in the middle of the mess for over an hour. "It would have been cheaper to charter a helicopter to take me back to my office," he muttered.

New York has always been uniquely different. As far back as the 1600's people came to New York to make money in any new enterprising way they could. An observant priest once reported that among its five-hundred inhabitants of that time there were at least twenty different languages being spoken largely due to New York being the only colony that was settled for economic reasons instead of religious ones.

As Corbin continued to glance around the city at the tall sky-scrapers and other buildings, it was hard for him to imagine, that at one time, where the buildings now stood, tribes of Indians roamed freely through the vast meadows, forests, and lands, planting tobacco, corn, wheat, and hunting wild turkeys, wild game, and scads of bountiful fish.

He shook his head in an attempt to bring his scattered thoughts back to the present after realizing the taxi driver had missed the proper turn off to his office. "What a perfect end to a won-da-ba morning," the agitated P.I. whispered, tapping on the protective window that separated the driver from the passengers.

"Turn right at the next light," he said.

CHAPTER 2

"No, No, Gabrielle. It's left, right, left, right, left. And, then it's left, right, left, right, hip! Try it again." Franco Morissette, famous dance coordinator from France snapped as he rolled his eyes, and stomped his stocking feet.

The fiery red haired dancer nodded, inhaled deeply, and took another stab at the dance routine, as she mumbled the dance steps rhythmically in her mind. Left, right, left, right, right, left, right, hip... Moments later, Franco was cursing under his breath again.

"Gabrielle, for Godssakes, this is not a difficult routine. Watch me again. And lovey, this time pay attention s'ilvousplait!" he barked, getting in her face and using two fingers to make quotation marks in midair.

The dancer nodded, stepped back several steps away from her instructor, and once again attempted to give him her complete attention.

"Left, right, left, right, left... Left, right, left, right, hip... Left, right, left, right, left... Left, right, left, right, hip! ... Got it?" he snipped, releasing a sigh of frustration.

The exotic dancer nodded waving her hands in midair. "Okay, okay. I think I got it. I can do this," she said with determination, as she watched Franco glance at his watch again.

THE SCARLET RIBBON —A one-of-a-kind girly club. It was far from a joint. It had high-dollar elegance and seduction subtly written all over the elaborately run nightspot for men.

The club was owned and operated by one time French playmate of the year Jacqueline Collins. Jacqueline was still stunning to look at. She held her forty-something age remarkably well. She still turned her fair share of heads.

After a long and bitter battle in the courts and thanks to the help of an unnamed source, Jacqueline finally won the palimony suit she had slapped on long-time multi-millionaire ex-boyfriend (and sugar daddy) Edward Stacy III.

She poured most of the money she had received from the palimony settlement into her long-time dream club The Scarlet Ribbon. The dancers were female, very lovely, very talented, and very sexy. They hailed from all over the globe, hand chosen by Jacqueline herself. Glowing reminders of her own youth. And most importantly, every single dancer had the exact shade of red hair color to match her own.

"Finally!" Franco squealed in relief when the beautiful young dancer mastered the complex dance step. He glanced at his watch with growing irritation. "Where the hell is she!" he complained, not noticing his boss standing attentively, watching directly behind him.

"Where's who, Franco?" Jacqueline asked, smiling and fondly patting the well-built dance instructor across his shoulders.

"Why Rachel Ward of course!" he barked, shaking his head. "I'd like to get out of here sometime before the show tonight. I have a life too ya know, Jacqueline!"

The glamorous club owner chuckled, understanding her gay friend's lack of patience. "Calm down, Franco. Apparently, Rachel's flight must've been delayed somewhere between France and here. It's nice of Rachel to fill in for Nikki on such short notice. So, be nice to her when she gets here, okay?" she playfully lectured, wagging her long, flaming red-colored fingernail in front of the ill-tempered dance instructor's face.

Franco placed his hands on his trim waist with arrogance. "I told you she should have taken The Concord."

Jacqueline shook her head in surrender as she curled her arm around the dance instructor's muscular arm, and led him in the direction of the bar. "Enough, Franco." She shrugged. "These things happen, you're just nervous about tonight's grand opening of the club. Is Dex coming tonight?" she asked, glancing up at Franco as they continued to make their way to the bar.

Franco waved his hand in the air and shrugged with uncertainty. "Who knows?" he answered tearfully, and cleared his throat. "Dex threw another one of his silly hissy-fits last night and stormed out of the house... I ... I just don't understand him anymore." He paused and swallowed. "That's why I'm so anxious to get home." He struggled hard to hold back his tears.

"I see." The club owner sighed, sliding herself onto a barstool. She glanced at her employee. "Calm down. I'm sure Dex will be there by the time you get home this afternoon. Let me buy you a drink. A Cuba Libre," she said to the bartender and then glanced at her watch.

Franco shook his head. "Make that a Strawberry Daiquiri," he injected reaching for a bar napkin to blot the corners of his eyes. "Jacqueline, do you really think Dex will be home when I get there?"

The former French playmate smiled and nodded. "Of course I do, Franco. After all, he hasn't had time to properly thank you for his new car yet, has he?" she said, shaking her head, and using her fingers as a comb to straighten her hair.

Franco nodded. He shoved a loose strand of hair out of Jacqueline's eyes. "True. But after I gave him the keys to it last night, instead of thanking me, he started a fight and took off in the damn thing," he whined reaching for his drink.

"What was the fight over?" Jacqueline asked, picking up her champagne cocktail.

Franco glanced at her with disbelief on his face. "Can you believe this? The goddamn color of the car. I ordered the damn thing in my favorite color. Call me silly if you want to, but I thought having the car in my favorite color would make Dex think of me every time he got into the damn thing. I was wrong." Franco sighed, reached for his drink and took a long sip through the straw.

The club owner bit her lower lip. "I see. So you had the car painted Magenta instead of?" She gestured with a roll of her wrist.

"Flaming red, of course. The shameless hussy," he snapped, before remembering that Flaming red was also the club owner's favorite color as well. "I'm sorry. No reflection on you intended. I'm just upset. You understand?"

Jacqueline chuckled. "No problem, Franco. Some people like it hot. While others simply do not," she countered as she picked up her drink. She took a sip and sat her glass on the bar.

"My point exactly. I'm just afraid Dex will go zooming all over the damn place advertising himself to the gay world," Franco spat in a jealous tone, drumming his fingers on the top of the bar.

"And you thought having the Viper painted Magenta would keep Dex closer to home?"

Franco shrugged his broad shoulders. "Something like that, I guess."

"Well Franco, my love, it's none of my business, of course, but maybe you should stop spoiling Dex so much. Sounds to me like he's becoming pretty…"

Franco stopped her. "Please Jacqueline. Don't say it. It's nothing I haven't thought of myself. Maybe you're right. Maybe I should remind him how dreadful his life was before I took his ass in and…"

The bartender interrupted their conversation to tell the club owner she had a telephone call. The same police detective had phoned for her earlier while she was out.

"Earlier?" A frown crossed her face.

"Yes. A homicide detective by the name of Charlie Miller." The bartender shrugged. "That's what he said, Ms. Collins."

"Thanks Dillon. Take the phone down to the end of the bar for me. I'll answer the call there," she said. "Wonder what that's all about, Franco?" She glanced at the dance instructor as she slid off the barstool. "I'll be right back," she said, "Have Dillon make us another drink."

She walked to the end of the bar and picked up the receiver. "Hello. This is Jacqueline Collins."

"Yes, Ms. Collins. This is Detective Charlie Miller. I'm with the New York City Police Department homicide division, ma'am."

"Yes, Detective Miller, what can I do for you?"

"I need to know if someone works for you by the name of Rachel Ward, ma'am."

"Why yes, Detective. Why?" she asked, tugging at the phone cord.

Detective Miller released a sigh of dread. "Ma'am, I need for you to come down to the city morgue. Ms. Ward was shot and killed at the airport this morning as she..."

"What?"

"I said..." The detective began again.

"No. I'm sorry, Detective. I heard you. It's just what you said was so shocking!"

"I understand Ms. Collins, but I need you to give us a positive I.D and some background information. Ms. Ward's closest of kin and..."

"Yes, of course. I'll meet you at the morgue in about thirty minutes. Will that be all right, Detective?"

"Fine. Thank you, Ms. Collins. I'll see you then." The detective said and hung up.

The stunned club owner heard the dial tone in her ear. She stood listening to the sound as she tried to pull her thoughts together. Several moments later, she released a sigh of utter disbelief and turned to face the dance instructor.

"Lovey, what is it?"

"Oh my God, Franco, it's Rachel. She's... She's dead!" she said, her tone trembling with emotion.

Victoria Taylor Murray

CHAPTER 3

Billionaire businessman Forrest Gray sat behind his six-foot long antique desk inside the study of his Greenwich Village Mansion. He was talking on the phone to the secretary of private investigator Corbin Douglas. Gray glanced at his gold Rolex before reaching for his cold cup of coffee. "And, what time do you expect Mr. Douglas to return, Ms. Fairbanks?"

"Ah, well, oh, ah... just a moment here he comes now Mr. Gray," she said, handing the phone to the P.I. when he reached her desk. She placed her right hand over the receiver as she whispered the billionaire's name.

Corbin nodded, accepted the phone receiver, and sat down on the corner of Marilee Fairbanks desk. "Forrest, I'm glad you called," he said, with a slight shortness of breath. He was still half-winded from running up the long flight of concrete steps leading into his office building.

"Did Ms. Rourke's flight make it in on time?"

"The flight was on time, but Ms. Rourke wasn't on it," Corbin replied.

"What? How can that be? I made all the arrangements last night myself." Forrest Gray exclaimed in disbelief.

"Well, maybe so. But Ms. Rourke wasn't on the flight."

"You're sure?"

"Yeah, I'm sure. The only redhead on the flight was shot and killed as she..."

"What?" The billionaire interrupted cutting the P.I. off in mid-sentence. "A shooting inside the terminal? I don't understand." He jumped to his feet, and paced around his desk.

"Yes. A red haired young woman by the last name of Ward. I don't know her first name." Corbin paused briefly, and then continued. "She was about the same age. A stunning resemblance actually."

With a heavy sigh, the billionaire sat down on the corner of his desk. "That sounds like Nikki's friend. Rachel Ward. They worked together from time to

10

time."

"You mean Ms. Ward was a professional dancer, too?" Corbin asked with interest.

Forrest released another sigh. "Yes. Apparently, Rachel must've been asked to perform at the new club that's opening in town tonight, too. The Scarlet Ribbon. That's why Nikki was coming to New York. She had promised a friend that she would help get the club off to a good start."

"What's the friend's name?"

"Jacqueline Collins, the famous French dancer and one time French play-mate of the year. Do you remember her?" The billionaire asked.

"Whew! Sure. A woman like Jacqueline Collins is hard to forget."

"Wonder why Nikki wasn't on the flight?" Forrest Gray's tone showed his concern.

"I was hoping you would be able to answer that question for me. I had to sit in traffic at the airport for over an hour this morning. And, on top of that my goddamn car got towed." Corbin said with an edge.

The billionaire gave an understanding sigh of apology. "Sorry. I'll have your car hocked out and brought to you," he offered, glancing at the time again.

"I've already made arrangements for that, but thanks for offering. So, what do you want me to do now?" The P.I. asked, as he motioned for his secretary to bring him a cup of coffee.

"I want you to find Nikki and keep an eye on her. That's what I want you to do, Douglas."

Corbin's mouth flew open with surprise. He shut it and said, "What? Surely you aren't suggesting I drop everything I'm working on, and haul my ass to France on the next flight out."

"I want her found!"

"I get the feeling there's something you're not telling me. What's going on?" Corbin asked, fumbling inside his shirt pocket for a cigarette.

"Listen. I know you're supposed to be the best P.I. in New York. Or, at least that's what..." He paused when his wife, Jill Jefferies Gray jerked open the door to his study.

"I'll have to phone you back," he said, in a rushed whisper, quickly hanging up.

Forrest Gray glanced at his wife. "Jill, how many times do I have to tell you not to come into my study without...?"

She interrupted him with a laugh. "Oh please, Forrest. Get a goddamn grip. I don't give a damn about your silly phone conversations. You were supposed to come downstairs and help me with the wedding plans for Sidney and Clay's..."

"I said I'd be down in a few minutes, Jill. There are things I need to attend to."

His wife stood just inside the study with her arms crossed above her waist, tapping her right foot. "You said that an hour ago. Now I must insist. The wedding of my best friend is in less than two weeks, and we have a lot to do. The wedding is our gift to them. I want everything to be perfect and…"

"All right. I don't understand why the hell you don't hire a wedding coordinator, and be done with it, for the love of…"

His wife silenced him with that special look of hers… a look that melted the very core of his being, even today, after twelve years of marriage. She smiled. "Be nice darling. I want to do this myself. It isn't like I have a million other things to do, is it?"

"All right. You win."

CHAPTER 4

It was a beautiful spring day darkened only by Corbin's increasing impatience with his latest client, Forrest Gray. "Why the hell doesn't he phone back!" he mumbled, glancing at his watch for the umpteenth time.

He slid his chair back and stood up walking over to glance out the large window in his office. As he stared down at the busy sidewalk of people, going back and forth in front of his midtown office building, across the street from Rockefeller Center, his thoughts drifted.

"Mr. Douglas, I have a cupcake assignment that I know you won't want to turn down. I know its short notice, but for a hundred grand you shouldn't mind the inconvenience too much..." His thoughts were interrupted when his secretary entered the office.

"Excuse me, Mr. Douglas."

Corbin turned and walked back to his desk. "Yes Marlee. What is it?"

"Mr. Gray phoned. He said to tell you that he was in the middle of something that was going to take a while. He would get in touch with you later. You also have Ms. Prescott on line one. And Detective Charlie Miller on line two."

Corbin cleared his throat. "Tell Regina that I'll phone her later. I'll take Charlie's call. Thanks Marlee."

"Charlie," he answered the call as he fumbled around his desk looking for a cigarette lighter.

"I just thought I'd call to let you know we got a positive I.D. on the redhead at the airport. Her name is Rachel Ward," he said, as he continued to scan the papers inside the file folder in his hands.

Corbin slumped back in his chair, and took a puff off his cigarette. "Who I.D.'d her?"

"Jacqueline Collins."

"The former French Playmate of the year and..."

Charlie cut in. "So, ya already know, huh?" He tossed the file folder down on his desk.

"Forrest Gray told me a little while ago."

Charlie shook his head and sighed. "So, Gray is your unnamed client, huh?"

"You are the clever dick. Aren't ya Charlie?" Corbin replied.

Charlie chuckled.

"What else do you have on Ms. Ward?" Corbin asked with interest.

"She hails from France, and was sent here to fill in for a Ms. Nikki Rourke, also from France. Apparently, both women are professional dancers, and…"

Corbin jumped in. "They came to New York for the grand opening of The Scarlet Ribbon."

"Your client told you that too?"

The P.I. smiled as he stubbed his cigarette out in the ashtray. "That's right, Charlie."

"Did he also tell you, the French authorities have a red-head murder on their hands? It happened last week inside the terminal at their airport. And, guess what else?"

Corbin sighed. "Another redhead?"

Charlie nodded as he picked up the folder again. "You guessed it!"

"I suppose she was also young, beautiful, and resembled Ms. Ward?"

"That's right."

"I wonder if it was the same shooter," Corbin mused with growing interest.

"Who said anything about this woman being shot?"

"You mean the other French babe wasn't shot?" Corbin's tone was one of surprise.

"I didn't say that."

Corbin fumbled inside his pocket for another cigarette. "Shit! I hate it when you do that, Charlie. Was she or wasn't she shot?"

"Okay, so the other redhead was shot too."

"Same gun?" the P.I. asked.

"I don't know yet. It's hard to say. But, sounds like it could be. There's a lot of similarities. I'm waiting to hear from the lab boys."

"A hit?"

Charlie shrugged. "Maybe."

"What else do you have?"

"Maybe some connection to your redhead."

"Nikki Rourke?"

"I wonder why she asked Ms. Ward to fill in for her at the last minute."

"I intend to find out," Corbin returned.

"Did your client tell you where she would be staying?"

Corbin shook his head. "Apparently she's still in France."

"Well, I could tell you what hotel she was originally registered to stay in but then you'd owe me big amigo!"

"Really? That's great, Charlie!"

"She hasn't checked in yet. She hasn't canceled yet either... But she did..."

Corbin stopped the homicide detective. "Shit Charlie! You're causing me stress here. But she what?"

"Keep it in your pants amigo! Apparently Ms. Rourke, or at least someone, phoned the hotel to check on her reservation this morning."

"So, are you going to tell me where, for chrissakes, Charlie?"

"Damn, Corbin! Maybe you should consider switching to decaf. She's registered at the St. Regis for the next two weeks. There. Are you happy now?" Charlie shook his head in playful dismay at his former partner.

"Thanks, Charlie. You may have saved me a goddamn trip to France," Corbin said.

"Wonder why your client never told you where she'd be staying?"

"Maybe he didn't make the reservations." The P.I. shrugged and then went on. "How did you find out so quickly, Charlie?"

"Jacqueline Collins told us."

"Do you think there's a possibility Ms. Rourke arrived in town this morning incognito?"

"You mean you think she deliberately..."

Corbin cut in. "Maybe she thinks someone is out to kill her, so she put on a disguise and went into hiding."

"You mean because of the young woman that was killed at the airport last week in France?"

"Yeah! And now Ms. Ward."

"Maybe she doesn't know about Ms. Ward yet, Corbin. If she wasn't on that flight how could she?"

"Maybe she used someone else's passport. You said yourself the three women look alike. Maybe she came in on the Concord."

"I'll check on it."

"Will you let me know if she checks in at the hotel?"

"If someone is trying to kill her, Ms. Rourke could be in danger."

"Yeah, I know. Wonder what's going on?"

"Your guess is as good as mine. Why did Forrest Gray hire you to tail her?"

"He didn't say. Guess I'll have another talk with him."

"Good idea. You'll keep me abreast of things, right?"

"Sure. We'll work together on this one. It'll be just like the good ole' days." Corbin chuckled.

"On second thought..." Charlie returned.

"Very funny Charlie. I need to hang up. I have a lot of work to do today."

"Adios amigo. I'll talk to you later."

Corbin dreaded the thought of having to cancel another date with his girl-friend, Regina Prescott.

Regina Prescott, high-priced and high-powered criminal attorney was lover to Corbin Douglas. Their fiery romance was as heated as some of the battles she waged in the courtroom.

After canceling his date with the female attorney, Corbin turned his atten-tion back to Nikki Rourke. As he slid the 8X10 photograph out of its yellow envelope, he also removed the retainer check for his services, and the young woman's brief bio... Nikki Rourke. Age twenty-six, emerald-green eyes, red hair, and, a body to die for.

"A body to-die-for indeed," he mumbled and stood. He grabbed his suit jacket dangling on the back of his chair, and hurried out of his office.

.

Chapter 5

Trump Towers. "Whew!" Corbin sighed, as his car sped past the luxurious hotel, thinking of Donald Trump. Now, that's who I want be when I grow up. He turned on the car radio.

Every channel had a different version of the early morning shooting at the airport. "Morons," he groaned and turned the radio off. His thoughts shifted... A beautiful face with a body to match. He was thinking about the lovely Jacqueline Collins as he continued his drive to The Scarlet Ribbon.

"Her Sugar Daddy must have been nuts to let a woman like her go," he mumbled, pulling his Stingray into the club's parking lot. He exited the car and moments later, he was inside the impressive new men's nightclub.

"Not bad!" he whispered, glancing around his surroundings unaware that the sexy club owner was walking up behind him.

"I'm glad you approve," Jacqueline said in a soft tone, adding, "Mister." It was an invitation for him to introduce himself. Her seductive gaze scanned the P.I.'s manly frame.

The Star-Struck private investigator returned a seductive smile, and eyed the long-legged beauty a moment before introducing himself to his longtime fantasy woman. "Douglas. Corbin Douglas."

"Mr. Douglas. I'm..."

Corbin stopped her with a knowing smile, and a nod. "I know who you are, Ms. Collins. I think the whole world does."

"Umm. Flattery. Women my age love that." She paused. "Especially, when it's coming from a sexy man like you, Mr. Douglas."

"Corbin. Please," he murmured.

"All right. In that case, call me Jacqueline. May I buy you a drink?" She gestured toward the bar area.

"Thanks. A Chivas on the rocks would be nice," he said, lowering his gaze to fully explore and enjoy the former French playmate's shapely figure, when she stepped in front of him to take the lead. Down boy! He silently scolded himself as the image of his girlfriend flashed a wagging finger at him.

The French dancer nodded to one of her two Italian stallions behind the massive marble and brass bar. "Dillon, bring me my usual, and Mr. Douglas would like a Chivas on the rocks." She smiled at the bartender before turning on her barstool to face the infatuated private detective.

"Now. What brings you to my new club, Corbin? The club doesn't officially open until this evening. The first show begins at nine."

"Yes, I know. But I need to speak with you about someone," he said, reaching for his drink.

"Oh? Who?"

"I believe she may be an employee. Nikki Rourke." Corbin sat his drink down and leveled his baby blues on Jacqueline's incredible emerald-green eyes.

The exotic dancer lifted her champagne cocktail, slowly putting the glass to her red lips. She took a small sip, as she seemed deep in thought. She finally responded. "Nikki? I see. Are you a police officer, Corbin?"

He smiled and shook his head. "No. I'm a private investigator." He picked up his drink.

Jacqueline sighed. "Sure. I remember now. I've seen your handsome face in the newspaper before. You're very famous," she said, placing her glass on the bar.

"I do all right." Corbin went on. "Nikki Rourke. Can we talk about her?" He motioned for the bartender to bring them another round.

"What is it that you want to know about Nikki?"

Corbin picked up his fresh drink. "Do you know where she is?"

Jacqueline shook her head. "No, I'm sorry I don't. She was supposed to be here to help me with the grand opening celebration tonight but she phoned last night and told me something came up. She said she was sending Rachel…" Her voice began to quiver. She reached for a bar napkin. "I'm sorry. I guess you've heard about Rachel?"

"Yes. I'm sorry. Pity. A beautiful, young woman like that." Corbin shook his head. "Do you know anyone who might've wanted to see Ms. Ward dead?"

Jacqueline sighed. "No. Rachel was a wonderful person. So young and full of life. She was a remarkable dancer."

Corbin shifted on his barstool. "I understand Ms. Ward and Ms. Rourke look so much alike they could almost pass for twins. Is that true?" He noticed the expression of sadness change to amusement.

"Corbin, all my dancers could pass for twins. I go to great pains to make sure…"

He cut in. "I get it," he admitted, blushing at his own stupidity.

She laughed. "All beautiful young women are glowing reminders of my own youth, you understand?" she said vainly.

"Umm. So it would seem," he offered, not knowing what else to say. He picked up his drink and took a long swallow.

She shrugged. "I travel the world over looking for fresh new talent so to speak."

The P.I. didn't comment on her remark about her world travels. Instead, he dove right into another question. "I understand both Ms. Ward and Ms. Rourke live in France. Is that correct?"

Jacqueline sat her empty drink glass down. "Yes, that's right. So does Atlantis and Katrina, my two real twin sisters. We call the twins Alley and Kat... Cute, don't you think?"

Corbin nodded. "Definitely. Was the young woman who was killed at the airport in France a week ago one of your dancers, too?"

Jacqueline sighed. "She had been at one time. That is to say, Camellia worked for me at a club I used to manage. That was about a year ago." She shifted her gaze back to her empty drink glass.

"Do you think there may be a connection to the two murders?"

"I have no idea, Corbin."

"Do you know anyone that might've wanted to see Camellia dead?"

Jacqueline shook her head with a decisive no, and finished her champagne cocktail. She nodded to the bartender to bring another round.

"What was Camellia's last name?"

Jacqueline looked at him as she spoke. "Villano."

"I thought you said Camellia was French?"

"She was... But her father is Italian— Rumor had it Camellia's father, Tommy Villano actually worked for the underworld at one time." Jacqueline offered as she tapped her long fingernail along the side of her glass.

"Really?"

Jacqueline nodded. "Yes. I never did comment on the rumor one way or another until now. But I personally believe those rumors to be true." She gazed with interest into the P.I.'s blue eyes.

"Do you know what the Mob Family's name was by any chance?" Corbin shifted his gaze back to his drink as he sensed the mature, but none-the-less sexy woman sitting beside him was subtly attempting to seduce him with suggestive glances.

She ran her index finger around the rim of her empty drink glass. "I believe the name you're inquiring about is the Juliano family. I think that family might've been from right here in New York. However, it could've been Chicago. I'm not sure anymore." She shook her head with uncertainty.

"I see."

Jacqueline glanced at her watch and squirmed on her barstool. Corbin noticed and smiled. "I hope I'm not keeping you from anything."

She returned the smile. "No, not really. I was about to ask you if you would like to join me in my studio apartment for a little while. I have a few hours to kill." She gazed with a lustful gleam into his eyes.

The private detective could feel himself becoming excited. A feeling that was new and disarming. He smiled. "I wish I could. But unfortunately, I can't. Not today anyway. A rain check perhaps?"

The former French dancer tossed him a playful pout of disappointment. "Anytime."

"Do you mind if I ask you a few more questions before I go?"

"Please do." She gestured her consent with a wave of her hand.

"Do you know anything about your employees' love interests?"

Jacqueline laughed. "You mean who they date and etc…"

"Exactly."

"Umm. That's a toughie, Corbin. I'm not at liberty to mention names. My customers are men of position, power and… well, you get the picture?" She seductively bit her lower lip and stared into his eyes.

"You mean married?"

"Something like that, yes."

He leveled his eyes to hers to better study her reaction to his next question. "Does the name Forrest Gray ring a bell?"

The red haired beauty flushed. She seemed to be choosing her words carefully. "But of course. He's very famous."

"And rich," Corbin interjected.

She smiled. "Yes, that too."

"He's a member of your club?"

"I know Forrest. Yes. We go back a ways."

"Lovers?"

"Maybe." A smile curled the corners of her lips.

"Do you know Mrs. Gray?"

Jacqueline gave a sarcastic chuckle. "Jill Jefferies Gray. Yes, I know of her."

"You've never met Mrs. Gray personally?"

"Why?"

"Just curious."

"Well, Detective, you know what they say about curiosity." Her tone was teasing.

"But Jacqueline…" Corbin paused, turned to face her, and added, "I'm not a cat."

"Purrrfect!" She laughed, shaking her lovely head at the same time.

Corbin chuckled at the club owner's cute sense of humor. "It was a pleasure meeting you, Jacqueline," he said as he stood up.

"As it was meeting you, Corbin. Please come back soon." She smiled suggestively.

"I will. Do you have a telephone I could use?" He glanced in the direction of the phone behind the bar.

"Don't tell me you're one of those people who have to check in every five minutes." A naughty grin crossed her face.

"Very funny, pretty lady, no, I'm not. Do you see a ring hooped through my nose? Or on this finger as far as that goes." He wiggled his ring finger in her face. "I just need to phone my secretary."

"I'd hate to think all the gorgeous men in the universe were married."

He chuckled, as she continued to flirt with him. "Are you always so forward in saying what you think?"

"Usually," she said, as her gaze traveled down the frame of his body, causing him to flush again. Damn! If only I wasn't in such a hurry, he thought, shaking his head with regret.

After a few heated moments of sexually charged silence, the club owner asked Dillon to bring the private investigator the telephone.

She rubbed her knee suggestively against the front of the P.I.'s trousers, causing an immediate reaction, as she leaned over to hand him the phone after Dillon placed it on the bar in front of her.

Blushing and instantly aroused, Corbin dialed his office, and asked his secretary to have one of his young detectives, Sam Maloney go over to the St. Regis Hotel and wait for a red haired young woman by the name of Nikki Rourke to check in. He also told his secretary that he was on his way to Regina Prescott's office. After spending the past hour or so talking to the seductive redhead, the P.I. knew his need for sexual release was great.

He replaced the receiver, smiled at the club owner and without saying a word, turned, and exited the elaborate nightspot for men.

Reaching the large glass front door to the club, he pulled it open and turned to glance back over his shoulder. He smiled at the incredibly sexy woman standing in the hallway with her arms folded, smiling at him in return. "Jesus!" he mumbled under his breath, as he fumbled inside his trouser pockets for his set of car keys. "Down Boy!" he scolded himself as he started his car.

Victoria Taylor Murray

CHAPTER 6

Jill Jefferies Gray raised her voice in excitement as she and her husband Forrest Gray entered the vast living room of their huge Victorian Mansion. "Oh, Mr. Carvalho, the gown is absolutely amazing... Don't you think, darling?" she exclaimed, glancing over her right shoulder at her husband.

Forrest nodded in agreement as his eyes traveled the length of the wedding gown and the young, attractive woman modeling it. "Yes, Jill, it is lovely. Sidney will look unbelievable in it," he returned, sneaking a brief glance at his watch.

His wife crossed the room anxious to get a better look at the gothic wedding gown. She spun the young model around in a full circle to better examine the beaded pearls, satin and lace. "Yes," she said, nodding with approval. "It's perfect. Absolutely perfect, Mr. Carvalho."

"Thank you, Mrs. Gray. I put my best effort into the gown. Well..." he paused briefly to reflect. "That is to say considering the short notice you gave me, madam."

Mr. Carvalho's arrogant tone was immediately noted by the billionaire businessman. He shot the famous designer a stern glance.

Jill smiled with apology at the arrogant designer. "Yes, I'm sorry about that. But you know how these things can just pop up right out of nowhere sometimes."

Forrest interrupted his wife's apology. "Darling please, you don't have to apologize or explain to Mr. Carvalho. Isn't that right, Mr. Carvalho?" he said, leveling his eyes at the famous, over-priced designer.

The designer's face instantly flushed. He cleared his throat and snipped, "Yes of course, Mr. Gray. But a little more notice would've been nice!"

The short-fused billionaire's mouth flew open in objection to the ill-mannered designer's continued arrogance. "Listen here Carvalho, one-hundred-and-fifty-thousand dollars for a little satin, lace and pearls should..."

His wife interrupted him. "Thank you, Mr. Carvalho. The gown is magnifi-

22

cent! We'll discuss the veil in a few moments." She smiled, nodded, and then turned to face her husband. "Forrest, stop it! Please. You're embarrassing me. This is supposed to be fun."

"I'm sorry, Jill. I don't have time for this today."

She sighed. "All right. Go! I'll take care of everything myself, Forrest. After all, this was my idea. But," she paused, and stared into her husband's eyes shaking her finger at him as she continued to speak. "I don't want to hear one word about what this wedding is costing. Agreed?" Her tone was firm. She began to tap her right foot, as she waited for her husband's response. A nervous habit she had picked up in her youth.

He gave a reluctant sigh of concession. "Fine, darling! Have it your way. Just remember we may decide to adopt a few children someday. And it would be nice if we could afford to send them to college," he remarked, lowering his head to kiss his wife on the cheek.

"Honestly, Forrest," Jill teased. "We could adopt fifty children, and our adopted children could have fifty children, and their children could have fifty children, and we would still have money to burn."

He smiled and turned to leave, as his wife continued. "You know what your problem is, Forrest?"

He stopped and turned to face her again. "No. What is my problem, darling?"

"You think holding onto your money will make you live forever."

Her husband chuckled. "What?" he exclaimed. "That's the most ridiculous thing I've ever heard. What woman's magazine did you get that information from? Oh, wait! Maybe it was one of those trash talk shows you love so much."

She shook her head. "Forrest, it doesn't work that way. The grim reaper can't be bought. When it's your time you're going to die just like everyone else."

The billionaire shook his head and laughed. "Gotta go. I'll call you later. Have a nice afternoon. Oh, by the way darling, where did you rush off to so early this morning?" He tilted her face and gazed into her eyes.

"Oh, ah… I'm sorry darling. I didn't mean to wake you. I had a few things I needed to take care of. You know, wedding stuff… And…"

He silenced her. "Never mind, you know how all this stuff bores me… I'm sorry I asked." He kissed her check again. "Bye darling."

Several moments later, he was back inside his large study. After several short business calls, the billionaire sent for his limo to be brought around to the back entrance.

"Good afternoon, sir." The chauffeur's son nodded, opening the door for the businessman.

A look of surprise crossed Forrest Gray's face. "Kyle? Where's Chapin?"

"Father had a few errands to run for Mrs. Gray. He asked me to sub for him."

"Whew! Poor Chapin. I'll be glad when this damn wedding is over. Jill's running everyone ragged." He shook his head. "It's been a while Kyle. You still working down at that Blues joint? What the hell is the name of that place, again?"

"The Blue Gibson. Yes. I'm still tending bar there. I'm working the split shift now though."

"I see." Forrest nodded.

"Where to, sir?" Kyle asked as the billionaire stepped inside the limo.

"I need to stop by the St. Regis first. Then I need to make a quick run to a new club that's opening in town tonight. The Scarlet Ribbon. Do you know where...?"

The chauffeur's son interrupted with a smile. "I know exactly where it is, sir," he said, closing the door. The young driver entered the stretch limo and started the engine. He glanced into the rearview mirror when he heard the dividing window slide down.

"Kyle, after the Scarlet Ribbon I'll need to stop by my Midtown office," Forrest said, glancing into the mirror at the young driver.

Kyle nodded as Forrest closed the glass window separating them. An instant later, the billionaire reached for the phone.

CHAPTER 7

"Damn it!" Hot-tempered female attorney, Regina Prescott spat under her breath, slumped back in her overstuffed chair, and hurled her long, legs up on top of the desk.

"That damn man of mine!" she cursed, leaning over to pick up a 5X7 photograph of him, sitting on her desk, with one hand, while she shoved her long blond hair out of her eyes with the other.

"Corbin, you jackass. It's the third time this week you've canceled a date with me, and I'm getting tired of it," she mumbled, outlining the smile on his face with her long, French manicured fingernail.

She kissed the glass where his lips were. "Whatever am I going to do with you?" she whispered, gazing at the picture with a sigh of resignation, and put the framed photograph back on her desk as her secretary, Sela Lawson entered.

"Here's the file on the Goodman case Mr. Davenport sent over this morning." She gazed at her employer. "Mr. Davenport also said to tell you, that he needed to see you in person. He would stop by sometime this afternoon."

Regina raised her eyebrows. "Oh, he did. Did he?" she replied, accepting the folder.

Her secretary smiled. "He did."

"Anything else, Sela?" she asked. There had to be something else; there was always something else with Kramer Davenport.

Sela nodded. "You guessed it. Another dozen red roses from the heartbroken Mr. Davenport were sent along with the Goodman file."

"Fabulous!" Regina sighed and rolled her lovely cobalt-shaded eyes. "I wonder what part of 'it's over, Kramer,' he doesn't understand?"

"Apparently, Mr. Davenport is still very much in love with you, Ms. Prescott," Sela offered with a shrug.

Regina chuckled. "Yeah, right. That's what he tried to tell me when I caught him in our bed with one of my best friends."

"All men make mistakes, Ms. Prescott. How can you not give him a second chance, he's so…" Sela's defense of her boss' ex-lover was silenced.

"Don't say it! Please," Regina interrupted. "You were going to say something about how good-looking Kramer is." She arched a quizzical eyebrow.

"God! I should be so lucky." Sela sighed.

"Yeah, I'll give him that much," Regina said. "Kramer is a babe all right. Not half-bad in the sack, either." She added with a grin.

Both women giggled, as Regina turned to see her boyfriend strolling unannounced into her office. Taken by surprise, she felt a warm flush creeping up her neck

"Corbin! This is a surprise." Regina cleared her throat. "I didn't expect to see you today." She rose to her feet as her secretary glanced at the P.I. and turned to leave.

"You don't have to leave on my account Ms. Lawson," Corbin said, stopping Sela before she reached the door.

She paused to face him. "I was about to leave anyway, Mr. Douglas."

Corbin turned his attention to his girlfriend. "What were you two ladies giggling about?"

Regina blushed again and shrugged. "Oh, just a couple of girls having a moment. You know… girl stuff."

"I see," he countered, smiling. "It wouldn't have anything to do with that bunch of red roses sitting on your secretary's desk that you received this morning from that old flame of yours, now would it?"

Regina stifled a smile. "So, you read the card?"

"I did. Does that bother you?"

"You don't see me snooping into your personal things do you, darling?"

He chuckled. "That's only because I haven't caught you, my dear."

"Why you …" He silenced her with a kiss.

Moments later, he pulled his lips from hers. "I want you, Regina," he whispered in her ear, his warm breath, sending goose bumps up her spine.

"Oh, God, Corbin!" she panted and pulled him back into her arms.

The telephone buzzed, spoiling a perfectly romantic moment. "Oh, that damn phone." Regina complained, reaching for the receiver.

She answered the intrusion with a chilly, "Yes?"

While his girlfriend was on the telephone, Corbin took a moment to do a little personal rearranging. Regina laughed into the receiver, when she noticed his right hand shoved down inside his tight-fitting trousers in an attempt to straighten his boxer shorts.

She cleared her throat. "Oh, I'm sorry Kramer. I wasn't laughing at you. It was Cor— Never mind. Please go on."

Corbin shook his head and gave a sexually frustrated sigh as he gestured to his girlfriend to hang up the phone.

She ignored his silent protest. "Shhh," she whispered, placing her hand over the receiver.

Corbin smiled and crossed the room to join her. She waited, knowing how much he wanted to have sex with her. Such a delicious thought.

He began to unbutton her silk, turquoise blouse with one hand as he nibbled up and down the nape of her neck and shoulders, his need for sexual release mounting.

Suddenly Regina's secretary entered the room and blushed at the erotic sight before her. "Excuse me, Ms. Prescott, Mr. Douglas. It's Judge Due. He says it's important. He's waiting in the lobby."

Regina cleared her throat and removed her hand from the covered phone. "Give me two minutes and then show Tom in," she said. "Listen Kramer, I have to go. I'll get back with you later." She hung up.

"Tom, huh?' Corbin frowned. His woman had called the shady judge by his first name.

Regina pulled him to her. "Oh honestly Corbin. Now be a good boy and run along before the judge walks in here and catches me with my blouse half off." She smiled mischievously and removed her arms from around his neck, buttoned her blouse and straightened her skirt.

"I guess that's better than getting caught with your trousers down," Corbin said, pulling her back into his embrace.

Judge Due had come storming into her office. He frowned at the two turned-on lovers. "Excuse me, Ms. Prescott, but I don't have any more time to waste while you two…"

Regina flushed and interrupted. "Ah, yes…your honor. Sorry. Corbin was just saying goodbye."

The shady judge leveled his angry gaze on the P.I. "Douglas," he said with a reluctant mumble, in spite of his dislike for the man.

Corbin nodded without speaking. He turned his attention back to his lover. "I'll call you later," he said, kissing her on the cheek.

Corbin nodded to Sela but she stopped him before he reached the door. "Oh, Mr. Douglas. You had a message from your secretary. She said to tell you to get down to the St. Regis Hotel A.S.A.P. Your red haired beauty just checked in."

"That's great," Corbin said as he rushed out the door.

CHAPTER 8

After receiving a second traffic ticket for speeding, Corbin Douglas finally pulled his recently restored Stingray up to the valet parking attendant at the St. Regis Hotel. Like a bolt of lightning, he exited the vehicle. Too lost in thought to speak to the valet, he nodded and whisked the claim check ticket from the young fellow's hand.

The beautiful St Regis Hotel is an elaborately restored beaux-arts gem, with elegant yet accessible public rooms and the finest service and amenities, second to none. People from all over the world come to enjoy the riches of Lespinasse, one of New York's top restaurants and the great King Cole bar dominated by the engaging Maxfield Parrish Mural of the king himself.

When the P.I. tried to enter the popular hotel, he was stopped at the entrance by two young uniformed police officers. One cop grabbed Corbin by his upper arm and said, "I'm sorry sir, but no one is allowed to enter or exit the hotel. There's been a murder inside one of the suites. You'll have to wait outside." The excited cop released his hand from around Corbin's right arm.

The P.I.'s mouth flew open in disbelief. "What? A murder?" he managed after he collected his thoughts. "Is Detective Miller here?" he asked, as the two cops prepared to enter the hotel lobby.

One cop nodded. Corbin smiled. "Good. Please tell the Detective that Corbin Douglas is here," he said, watching from out of the corner of his eye as people attempted to squeeze past him.

The two cops stopped their efforts. "Sorry folks, you can't come in here. You'll have to wait outside," one said, glancing in Corbin's direction. He shook his head with irritation. "I don't mind relaying your message, Mr. Douglas, but you'll have to watch the door for me for a few moments, okay?" He motioned for one of the bellboys to come and help hold the people at bay.

"No problem," The P.I. said turning his attention to the small mob of curious people. Then he noticed a young man with wavy blonde shoulder-length hair glance over his shoulder and shed what appeared to be a waiter's jacket. He was walking across the busy street. He slid into a shiny-black limo, and without hesitation pulled it out into traffic. In a moment, the limo disappeared from view.

"Damn," Corbin mumbled under his breath. He felt envious that he couldn't drive like that, especially in a city the size of New York.

The police officer returned and said, "Detective Miller wants you to go up. He's on the thirteenth floor. Suite 1333. By the way, Mr. Douglas, didn't you used to be a co..."

Corbin cut in. "Yes I was."

"Man, this is an honor. There's been a lot of talk going on about you for some time, now. You're a legend down at the station, sir." The young cop said, sharing a quick glance at his partner while he extended his hand to the P.I.

Corbin shook the cop's hand and chuckled. "A legend? I wouldn't go that far." With a nod, he darted inside the hotel seeking the nearest elevator.

Once inside the elevator, he pressed the button for the thirteenth floor. The door slid shut and began its journey upward, stopping once at level seven to allow a very attractive woman in her early to mid-thirties to enter.

The young woman ignored the friendly nod of the P.I. as she continued to talk on her cell phone. Corbin's gaze traveled the length of the woman's frame. Umm...both, attractive and rich. He thought glancing at her ring finger to see if she was married.

"All right Kyle, for chrissakes! If I have to drag her down there myself by the hair of her head, I will. I swear. Stop worrying... The Blue Gibson in lower Manhattan. Across the street from what used to be The World Trade Center...I got it. We met there, remember? Okay...Okay... Kyle, Geese." The woman snapped to whomever she had been talking to as she stepped off the elevator on the thirteenth floor still clutching her cell phone as though it were a priceless gem.

Corbin shook his head and stifled a chuckle as he stepped off behind her. He almost bumped into her when she froze in her tracks, after seeing the commotion going on. She turned to face the P.I. Her face was a noticeable mask of white, showing an unmistakable touch of fear. Corbin observed her reaction though she was wearing her oversized designer sunglasses.

"Oh my God!" she squealed. "I...I must have gotten off at the wrong floor by mistake." She rushed back inside the elevator and stood tapping her right foot impatiently as she waited for the elevator door to close.

The P.I. continued to watch until the elevator door closed and began its long journey downward. He glanced over his shoulder as he walked away curious to see if the elevator stopped on the seventh floor where she had initially boarded it. But the elevator didn't stop. He shrugged and turned to enter suite 1333.

CHAPTER *9*

New York crime boss Anthony Juliano and foot soldier Carmine 'Blade' Asaro sat in the back seat of the underworld figure's shiny, black limo parked across the street from the St Regis Hotel. They stared at everyone who tried to enter the hotel.

"I don't fucking care how much it costs, I want that broad iced, got it Blade? The next time you and I see one another the goddamn broad better be sleeping with the pesce capisce?"

Carmine nodded, understanding the underworld figure's threat. An instant later Carmine spotted the young woman they had been looking for.

"Shit! There she goes, boss! Dare un`occhita. (Take a look)."

The Mobster's gaze followed the bouncing redhead as she entered the hotel lobby.

"Just make sure it's the right goddamn broad this time, Carmine, or it might be you that winds up sleeping with the fish, capisce? Now get the fuck out of here. I don't want to see your ugly ass until the job is done."

Carmine released a frustrated sigh. "Calm down Anthony. I'll take care of it. I'll take care of everything. Don't worry about it." Carmine opened the limo door, spat, and slid out. "I'll call you later," he said, closing the door.

The mobster slapped the back of the driver's seat with his leather glove. "Let's get the fuck out of here, Sonny.

Anthony J. Juliano was New York City's notorious bad boy with a capitol 'B'. He was a striking man in his late forties, who had the build and strength of a man in his late twenties. He was good looking, jet-black hair, and noble features. He was also well endowed and fancied himself quite a ladies man.

Anthony Juliano was also a ruthless cold-blooded killer. A monster in every sense of the word. He had connections all over the world, political and other-wise. He was a man who earned his billions the old-fashion way – killing, stealing, and extortion. And of course, using people. He ran most of the lower eastside including Chinatown. Whore houses, gambling joints, and of course, drug houses.

Anthony also dabbled in the stock market, and owned shares of AT&T, TWA, and numerous other legal stocks, as well as numerous legitimate companies and corporations. He employed thousands of people in both his legitimate enterprises as well as his illegal affairs. The mobster was not a man to cross. On his way up in the ranks of the underworld, Anthony murdered many people. Men and women. And even a few children along the way. He also ordered the deaths of hundreds of other people for profit and gain. Or, to save his own skin.

Anthony had a criminal record that went as far back as his childhood. He had been arrested twenty-two times for various criminal offenses, but oddly, for the past ten years the charges had always managed to be dropped — generally due to evidence suddenly vanishing into thin air or a disappearing witness.

The F.B.I. had spent the past five years placing undercover agents inside Anthony's organization. Some agents disguised as 'fixers' and 'money movers'. A 'fixer' excelled in developing contracts with criminal justice or political officials and when necessary, he arranged for corruption. The 'money movers' were experts at laundering illicitly obtained money, disguising its origin through a string of transactions and investing it in legitimate enterprises.

Gambling, even though most states had legalized it in its many forms, remained one of the mobster's most lucrative means of illegal money gain. Especially in the lower eastside. Narcotics, loan sharking, extortion, and labor racketeering net the underworld crime family billions of dollars a year as well. The ill-gotten billions were laundered through his many legitimate industries — reality, labor unions, securities, restaurants, nightclubs, gas stations, clothing outlets, and boutiques as well as the manufacturing of these garments and Waterfront districts, disposers of garbage, and vending machine operations.

In the near future, the F.B.I. hoped to have enough evidence on Anthony Juliano and his underworld organization to put him away forever, and put the organization out of business permanently.

*****

The two photographs of Rachel Ward plastered across the front page of the New York Sun gave Jill Jefferies Gray the creeps when she glanced at the headlines, as she walked past the rack after leaving Tiffany's. She had gone to the exclusive department store to register her friend Sidney's upcoming marriage. Her selection at the famous store – Tiffany's Audubon Silver Pattern and Limoges China.

Serves the slut right. The billionaire's wife thought as the image of the dead woman replayed repeatedly in her mind. Too bad, it wasn't Forrest's newest fling. She continued deep in thought while she tried to flag down a taxi. The quick stop she had made at Tiffany's had made her late for her pre-arranged luncheon date.

*****

"Hello Scottsdale. I'd like to speak with Mrs. Gray please," Forrest Gray said to his butler who answered the telephone at his estate.

"I'm sorry Mr. Gray, but Mrs. Gray said she had a few errands to run this afternoon."

"Did Chapin drive her to town?"

"No sir. Mrs. Gray insisted on taking a taxi."

"What?" Forrest sighed in frustration. "All the goddamn automobiles just sitting around the estate and Jill wanted to take a taxi? I don't believe it Scottsdale." He sighed again and glanced at his Rolex. "What time did my wife say she would be home?"

"She didn't, sir. Is there a message?"

The billionaire glanced at his wife's photograph sitting on the desk in his Midtown office.

"No, thank you. Just tell Mrs. Gray that I telephoned."

"Will that be all, sir?"

"I'm curious Scottsdale, how long did the preparations go on this morning for Ms. Cox wedding plans?"

"Not long at all. Ms. Gray sent everyone away right after you left, sir."

Forrest looked thoughtful for a moment before responding. "Really?"

"Yes sir. Said she remembered something important she needed to attend to."

"I see. Okay. I'll be home in a few hours if she should call." Forrest hung up the phone, wondering where his wife had rushed off. What could have been so important she felt the need to take a taxi?

*****

After hailing a taxi, Jill Jefferies Gray glanced at her watch with a slight cringe followed by a small sigh of frustration.

"Where to, miss?" The cabbie asked, after the wealthy woman let herself inside and slammed the door.

She gave the taxi driver a nasty look. "Geeze! You fella's don't bother helping a lady inside the taxi's anymore, huh?" she snapped, making eye contact with the cabbie through his rearview mirror.

The taxi driver ignored her remark. "Like I said miss, where to? I ain't got all day." He scratched the side of his head and pulled his cab out into the traffic.

"You can drop me off on Park Avenue. The Waldorf Astoria. And if you don't mind, I'm running late, so step on it."

*****

The famed Waldorf-Astoria Hotel, far grander than the original Waldorf, is residence for many who are rich and or famous. Royalty and presidents alike. Its luxurious art deco marble-columned lobbies filled with bronze and mahogany. A highlight is 'The Wheel of Life.' 1931. A one-hundred-forty-eight-thousand piece tile mosaic depicts the drama of human existence by French artist Louis Rigal.

CHAPTER 10

A small army of experts was examining the crime scene as Private investigator Corbin Douglas entered the posh hotel suite.

The forensic specialist, the medical examiner, crime photographer, fingerprint lifters, serologists, and white glove experts were vacuuming for hair, dust, and carpet samples, doing whatever they could to search-out evidence that might have been left during or after the murder. Clues. Turning the luxurious suite inside out. 'A scene I am well used to. That is to say if anyone could actually get used to such a sight.' Corbin thought, shaking his head.

"Corbin! Over here," homicide Detective Charlie Miller called. He was stooped over the body of a dead woman. "Is this the young woman you been trying to track down all morning?" he asked.

Corbin shook his head, and offered the detective a hand up. "No, Charlie. That's not her."

Charlie stood up. "You're sure?" He scratched the side of his head thoughtfully.

Corbin nodded. "Yes, I'm sure. That woman is not Nikki Rourke."

"Well, according to the front desk clerk this is the woman who entered the hotel and registered as Nikki Rourke a few hours ago," Charlie returned.

Corbin glanced around the room. "This case is getting stranger by the minute, Charlie. How did she die?"

"Gun shot to the back of her head, just like that redhead at the airport this morning."

"The two murders seem to be related."

"It looks that way. Oh, and for the record, better make that three murders. The one in France, same M.O." He sighed. "It's starting to look as though someone wants Nikki Rourke dead, real bad!"

"Yeah, it looks that way," the P.I., agreed. "What do you have, Charlie?" Corbin asked.

Charlie shrugged. "Not much," he said. "Looks like a professional hit though."

"How so?" Corbin asked.

"Bada-Bang. It's over. Clean, neat, to the point. The killer, quick in, quick out. Must've used a silencer."

Corbin nodded toward the dead woman. "Wonder who she is?"

"My guess?"

"Yeah."

"Another professional dancer, I would imagine."

"Did you send for Jacqueline Collins?"

Charlie shook his head. "Nope, not yet. Thought I'd send someone for her after we take the body to the morgue. What about you, you got anything yet?"

"Nothing solid," Corbin replied.

"How did you hear about this so quickly?"

"I didn't. I had Maloney waiting downstairs for Ms. Rourke to check in. Sam saw the mystery redhead check in and thought it was Nikki Rourke. He phoned, I hightailed it down here."

"What now?"

"I think I'll give my client another call."

"Let me know what he has to say."

Corbin nodded. "Sure thing," he said, and turned to leave.

"Before I forget, do you want to go to the grand opening of The Scarlet Ribbon with me tonight?" Charlie asked.

"You think Ms. Collins will…"

Charlie interrupted his friend. "Yes, she will want to open the club tonight, anyway. I already suggested she hold off on the opening celebration until after we figure out what the hell is going on. She said she couldn't postpone it. Says she got club members coming in from all over the globe tonight."

"Yeah, but now there has been three young woman murdered, and all three have connections to her."

"How do you know that, Corbin?"

"Three dancers. Three redheads. Three…"

"How do you know the young woman in France even knew Ms. Collins?"

"I talked to Ms. Collins this afternoon."

"Anything I should know about?"

"We'll talk later, Charlie. Not here. The walls could have ears, if you know what I mean."

"Sounds interesting."

"Could be something."

"You'll meet me at The Scarlet Ribbon tonight then?"

Corbin nodded. "Yeah, unless I run into my client's beautiful, young mistress," he said, with a smile.

"About nine o'clock then?"

"Nine o'clock it is. I'd better rocket," Corbin said, glancing at his watch. "See you later, amigo."

Corbin stood aside to let the medical examiner pass with the stretcher holding the young woman's body. "Yeah, later, Charlie," he said, following behind the small group of experts.

Before Corbin left the hotel, he stopped at the pay phone to make a few calls.

CHAPTER *11*

"I was thinking perhaps an English, fourteenth-century wedding. What do you think Sidney?" Jill Jefferies Gray asked, motioning for the male waiter to bring another bottle of red Bordeaux.

"You mean a Camelot wedding? Like King Author and Guinevere?" The bride-to-be quizzed.

Jill nodded and sat her wine glass down. "Exactly," she said.

The wedding coordinator from Gateau de Mers, Tinker French, jumped into the conversation. "That's a wonderful idea!"

"Wonderful? You mean romantic don't you, Ms. French?" Jill asked, with a chuckle.

"Will the Gothic theme go with my wedding gown, Jill?" Sidney asked.

Jill sipped her wine. "Yes, of course. That's why I held off on the veil. I wanted to make sure you liked the idea first."

"What's not to like? I love it, but we have such little time to put it all together."

"I'm more concerned with how you're going to talk Clay into wearing a pair of tights, a cape, and tunic," Jill replied, with a giggle.

After the three women shared a hearty laugh, Jill lifted the wine bottle and refilled their glasses. "Tinker, I'll tell you how I imagine things should be and then you put it all together for me. Whatever I don't mention or can't think of — take it upon yourself to include. Everything must be perfect, but remember, it's very important for my husband to think I arranged everything in Sidney's wedding. Is that understood?"

The gay wedding coordinator nodded. "But, of course, Mrs. Gray. My lips are sealed," she assured.

The billionaire's wife shifted her gaze and wagged her finger in her friend's face. "And, that goes for you too, Sidney. Not a word to Forrest about the wedding coordinator I hired. I had to promise him that I would handle everything myself to get him to pay for it, okay?"

Sidney nodded her agreement to her wealthy friend. "All right, but I still don't understand why all the secrecy Jill. You know as well as I do that Forrest lets you have anything you want." She shrugged and sipped her wine.

Jill smiled. "That's true. Generally anyway, but to tell you the truth, Forrest doesn't like Clay that well."

Sidney's mouth flew open in disbelief, but just as quickly, she closed it. "What? But why?"

"When Clay backed out of the deal Forrest set up for him last year he..."

Sidney cut in. "Never mind. That's water under the bridge. Let's get back to the wedding shall we?"

"All right. You're sure Clay will go along with the theme of things?" Jill asked, finishing her wine.

"You worry about the wedding arrangements and I'll take care of Clay."

Tinker French pointed to her briefcase. "Is it okay if I get my tape recorder out, Mrs. Gray? It will save the time and trouble of taking notes."

"Not a problem," Jill said, as she motioned for the waiter, raising her empty wine glass. The waiter nodded his understanding.

Tinker French removed the tiny tape recorder from her brief case and turned it on. "Okay, I'm ready Mrs. Gray. Shoot."

Jill looked thoughtful as the waiter set a full wine bottle on the table. "Let's see." She waved her right hand in midair, a habit she had while talking. "We'll need the invitations to go out immediately. Hire a calligrapher to make scroll-type invitations. Old English writing, of course. I want the pieces of parchment rolled, put in tubes, and sealed in wax with the wedding couple's initials." She paused as she poured new wine into her glass. "I want the calligrapher to tie purple and gold velvet ribbons around the tubes. And don't forget to request that all royal guests wear theme clothing in colors of purple and gold," she said, and sipped her drink.

Sidney touched her friend's arm. "You have given this wedding a lot of thought haven't you, Jill?"

Jill nodded.

"Would you describe the wedding gown for me please, Mrs. Gray?" Tinker asked.

"Certainly. It's a close fitting gown, coterharide if you will. It has a scoop neckline, long, tight fitting sleeves, full skirt starting below the hipline and of course, a long train attached at the shoulders. As far as the veil, I was thinking along the lines of perhaps a jeweled crown instead. The gems would match the main color in the scheme of things. I thought maybe a rainbow of colors unless you would like to stick to the usual stones found in most crowns. What do you think Sidney?" Jill turned her attention to her friend.

Sidney looked thoughtful for a moment and then shrugged. "You choose,

Jill. You're running the show."

"All right Sidney. I believe the color sliver is in the coteharide. We'll go with that. Ms. French, I want you to telephone Mr. Carvalho and give him my selection. And tell him that I have decided to have him make all the costumes for the wedding party. You'll have to personally make all the arrangements, time, schedules, fittings and etc., between everyone and Mr. Carvalho."

Tinker French nodded. "Fine. And what do you want to do about the bridal bouquet?"

Jill looked thoughtful. "I doubt Sidney will go for the traditional white bible of that time period so we'll go with the flower bouquet," she said, with a chuckle. "But remember to have the florist go heavy on the silver ribbon," she added.

"All right. Now for the groom's attire," Tinker said.

"Well, like I said before, Ms. French, the groom will have to dress according to that time period. You know sort of like that movie that was out a few years back starring Richard Gere. That Camelot movie. What was the name of it?"

"Oh, I remember," Sidney, exclaimed. "The First Knight. God, he's so hot, don't you think, Jill?"

Jill poured more wine. "Who? Richard Gere?"

Sidney rolled her eyes in playful dismay. "Duh!" she teased. Jill and Tinker laughed.

"Yes, Sidney. Richard Gere is a babe all right. You know now that I think about it, don't you think Clay favors him? I mean honestly, Clay could almost pass for his twin brother," Jill said, shaking her head in amazement.

"Oh, my gosh! Clay does look like him, doesn't he?" Sidney exclaimed, again causing Jill and Tinker to laugh.

"Umm, well Richard Gere may be a babe, but I still can't believe he let Cindy Crawford get away from him that easily. Men, geeze!" Jill said, shaking her head in disdain.

"Hey, that's not a fair thing to say, Jill," Sidney scolded. "Who said he called it quits with her? Maybe she left him. After all, she's the one who rushed right back into marriage again with someone else. And now she's even a mother. Babies. Gee aren't they…"

"Ladies, can we please get back to the wedding arrangements," Jill interrupted. "The last thing I want to discuss right now is children for goodness sakes!"

"Sorry!" Sidney shrugged. "But I like babies. I thought you liked children too, Jill,"

"Sidney, just remember this. Once you have a baby, you won't be the baby anymore. Now, let's get back to the wedding. Where were we?"

"You were saying …'

"Yes, I remember. We were discussing the groom. The groom will wear a long, knee-length tunic, tights, and knee-length, leather boots. And, of course,

Clay will need a long flowing cape that ties in the front like a robe. The colors should compliment Clay's sexy royal-blue eyes."

"Good choice, Mrs. Gray. What color would you like the trim to be around the tunic?" Tinker asked.

"Let's go with black. Very manly, don't you think?"

Sidney nodded. "Very," she slurred, glancing around for the waiter.

Jill waved him over with another bottle of wine. "Geeze, the service in this place today is impossible!" Jill snapped, glancing at her watch. "Not the usual norm for The Waldorf."

Sidney shook her head. "I agree," she replied.

Jill released a heavy sigh. "Okay, now let's discuss the groom's men." She looked thoughtful for a moment and then continued. "Of course, they must dress similar to the groom, but without the cape. Perhaps, we should have Mr. Carvalho add arm shields and a coronet to look more the part. Same colors as the groom but reverse them. You know what I mean, black tunics with royal-blue trim."

"And the bridesmaids?"

"They'll dress similar to the bride, of course, but go with the color in the coteharide. We want silver, I believe," Jill said, as she tasted her wine and then waved the waiter away. "Oh, don't forget, no train for the bridesmaids. You'll have to hire a few beauticians for makeup and hair. The bridesmaid's hair will be braided with beaded jewels. And, don't forget, they are to carry the bride's train down the wedding aisle."

The wedding coordinator removed the tape and popped in a new one. "Now for the flower girl," she said, smiling.

"I believe Clay told me that he wanted his twin nieces to do the honors. Dress the four-year old twins like the bridesmaids. The only difference will be I want the twins to wear cone-shaped veiled hats. Mr. Carvalho might want to add a few colored beads at the tip of the veil. The girls will, of course, spread fragrant rose petals along the bridal path," Jill said, glancing at the time again.

The wedding coordinator reached for her glass of wine. "And the ring bearer?" she asked.

"Well, let's see." Jill paused and then went on. "Dress the groom's younger brother as a page. Same colors as the groom, but his cape will be shorter, tights, boots, and an over-sized floppy hat, too. The ring bearer is to be given a rolled scroll tied with velvet ribbon and attached to the ribbon will be the wedding bands." She smiled. "Well, what do you think ladies?"

Tinker French shook her head. "I'm amazed. You're a natural born wedding coordinator, Mrs. Gray. I couldn't have planned this wedding any better myself. I'm impressed!"

Jill smiled. "Thank you, Ms. French. I have to admit I have given this wedding a lot of thought, time, and energy."

"What about the church, Jill?" Sidney asked.

"Well, I haven't given the church a lot of thought. I mean, I know how I see it decorated in my mind, but I haven't called any of them. You'll have to do that. But the church should be gothic-style of course. Hire some actors as guardsmen. They should be instructed to form a tunnel with their swords for the wedding processional. They too will be dressed in tunics, tights, boots, etc... And don't forget they should wear gauntlets and helmets as well."

Jill picked up her drink and went on. "The church should be decorated fitting the theme of the wedding, candles along the alter, flower garlands along the sides of the seats or benches. And you might want to consider placing a few torches in tall iron stands going down the aisle."

Tinker nodded. "And, what would you like in the way of music?"

Jill looked thoughtful and downed the last swallow of her drink. "Hire some bagpipe musicians to lead the wedding processional and a bugler to announce the royal couple. In place of the usual rice throwing or bubbles, I want you to locate a confetti cannon. I believe this hotel used one of those type machines a few years ago at a New Year's Eve party I attended. It was either here or Trump Towers." She sighed remembering the happy event. "Be sure and arrange for a horse and carriage fancied up, of course. I want them to take the newlyweds on a quick trot through Central Park before bringing them to the hotel for the dinner party. You'll have to get with the banquet manager here at The Waldorf. I want them to transform the ballroom into a romantic Camelot. Hire all the actors you think you might need to greet the guests as they enter the grand ballroom. Make sure management understands the theme of the wedding party. I want the hired help appropriately dressed, and I want them told to use phrases like; 'your majesty' and etc..." Jill said, glancing around the restaurant. Suddenly she noticed her chauffeur's son sitting at the bar flirting with a young cocktail waitress. Shit! She thought glancing at her watch.

"Geeze, can you believe the time, it's almost dark," she said. "I think I'll go powder my nose and give Forrest a call. I bet he's wondering where I am. Scottsdale probably told Forrest I left right after he did this morning. You know what a big mouth our butler has," Jill said, standing. "Oh, shit!" she added, reaching for the edge of the table to steady her wobbly legs. "I think I'm getting a little tipsy, Sidney. How about you?" she asked with a giggle.

Sidney giggled too. "I passed tipsy after the second bottle of wine." She smiled. "You want me to go to the ladies room with you, Jill?"

Jill chuckled again. "No thanks. I think I can make it on my own. I'm tipsy, not drunk Sidney," she returned. "Why don't you order us another bottle of wine, and I'll be back in a few minutes."

CHAPTER *12*

The early afternoon luncheon date Jill Jefferies Gray was having with her long time friend Sidney Cox had somehow turned into more than Jill had bargained for. "Geeze," she moaned as she attempted to straighten her tight fitting skirt and matching tangerine-colored suit jacket. "Damn," she complained, noticing a few unsightly splashes of red wine on her expensive silk blouse created especially for her by famous, French clothing designer, Perrier DuVall. Jill washed her hands, and fluffed her long red hair. 'Well, at least I look sober enough,' she thought, returning her tube of lipstick to her purse.

Then she remembered an important stop she wanted to make before going home. Jill found her pen and scribbled a note to her friend, apologizing for the rude departure, saying that the luncheon tab had been taken care of, to stay as long as she and Ms. French liked, and she would phone her friend at home later that evening. Jill rushed out of the ladies room and ran head-on into a cocktail waitress. The experienced cocktail server managed to avoid what could have been a small disaster by raising the tray high above her head. "Whew, close call," the server murmured with a sigh of relief.

"I should've been paying more attention to where I was going. Sorry. Are you all right?" Jill asked, as she glanced in the direction of her friend and the wedding coordinator from Gateau de Mers.

"I'm fine, Mrs. Gray. Maybe just a little shaken."

"Good." Jill smiled. She handed the young woman the note and pointed in the direction of her friend's table. "Would you be kind enough to hand this note to my friend, Ms. Cox? She's the lady that's trying to get the server's attention. And, please tell our server to put everything on Mr. Gray's tab. Also, tell the waiter I said to add a little something on, in the way of a tip for you as well. Okay?"

"Yes, certainly Mrs. Gray. Thank you very much." The server smiled as Jill walked away.

The Shadow of Her Smile

*****

When Corbin Douglas rounded the corner of Fifth Street in his Stingray, he saw a woman who looked familiar. But he couldn't be sure she was the same woman who had entered the elevator at the seventh floor of The St. Regis Hotel earlier in the day. This woman wasn't wearing a large floppy hat or designer sunglasses. He continued to watch as she attempted to flag down a taxi. When she began to tap her right foot impatiently, Corbin was convinced that it was her. Curious about the shapely redhead, Corbin decided to follow her as he remembered the scared look on her face when she saw commotion occurring inside suite 1333.

Her first stop was at a bank. She went inside for a few moments. Her next stop was Sotheby's.

Corbin parked his Stingray across the street from the world-renowned auction house and entered shortly after his lady of mystery. She seated herself in the front row, and Corbin sat down several rows behind her.

"It's just the cutest little painting. I must have it!" Corbin heard her say to the woman seated beside her. Moments late, the auction began.

"The bidding will start at one-hundred-thousand dollars. This armchair was made in 1760 right here in New York. As you will notice, it has a ruffled splat and eagle's head. The seat is upholstered, leaf carved cabriole legs, and ball and claw feet. Do I hear one-hundred-twenty-five-thousand dollars?" the auctioneer said with insistence. Something apparently he was good at, Corbin thought, as he glanced around the room. Moments later, Corbin's mystery lady was the proud owner of the three-hundred-eighty-seven thousand dollar chair. 'Without a doubt, the ugliest chair I have ever seen in my life. Unbelievable!' Corbin shook his head in dismay.

The next item the P.I.'s lady of mystery purchased was a Queen Anne easy chair with walnut legs and stretchers, made in Boston in 1740. She paid an astonishing three-hundred-thousand dollars for that piece of furniture. Corbin sat dumbfounded, shaking his head in total disbelief, curious as to just who his lady of mystery was, and how she could sit there, and so effortlessly keep nodding her lovely head in agreement to each bid the auctioneer asked for, seeming determined to outbid everyone else.

Her next purchase was a necklace. A whopping nine-hundred-forty-thousand dollars. The flabbergasted P.I. could hardly contain himself. It was the most ridiculous piece of jewelry he had ever seen in his life. "Jadeite jewelry," the auctioneer said proudly. He went on. "A single strand jadeite-bead necklace from the stone 'Doubly Fortunate', twenty-seven matched jadeite beads, approximately five-eights inches each in vivid emerald color with old European cut diamond terminals. Eighteen and one-half inches long, to the diamond, single-stone clasp."

The wealthy mystery woman's final purchase was a man's Patek Philippe yellow-gold wristwatch, with matt silver and applied gold indexes, perpetual calendar, and moon phases. Made in 1961. The cost to Corbin was a mind blowing one-million dollars that she paid.

"I'm telling you Charlie, I couldn't fucking believe it!" Corbin said in the phone to his friend.

Charlie coughed.

"The woman is loaded. I have no idea who she is, but I intend to find out. What? Did I buy anything?" Corbin repeated his friend's question. He chuckled shaking his head. "Well sure. A little something. I didn't want to look out of place. What huh?" he said, with another chuckle. He paused to light a cigarette, as he glanced over his shoulder at his attractive surveillance subject, and then turned his attention back to his phone call.

"Yeah, I was getting to that. But you have to promise not to laugh," he said. "I bought a lure fisherman's box, Charlie. What? No, it's not a goddamn Bat Masterson's!" he snipped with irritation. "It's a Red fin Floating Bart box with label. A Casting and Trolling Bart for Bass and Pickerel. What? Okay, I'll tell you the price, but you have to promise not to make fun of me, okay?" he said, glancing over his shoulder at his mystery lady again.

"Three-thousand-nine-hundred-sixty dollars."

Corbin felt his face flush when his friend began choking and laughing at the same time.

Corbin shook his head. "Calm down Charlie. It's only money. I have to go. My mystery woman is on the move. Yes, I remember. Tonight at nine o'clock," he said, and clicked off his cell phone.

Chapter 13

The huge cast iron lock was broken on the iron gate; allowing Nikki Rourke to enter her grandmother's run down estate with little effort.

It had been almost three years since her last visit to the estate. A sad occasion. Her grandmother's funeral. Nikki released a sigh of regret as she passed through the rusty old gate. It squeaked and slowly closed behind her.

Through the beautiful century old trees at the end of the cobblestone driveway, she could see the main house. A comforting sight, considering all Nikki had been through the past twenty-four hours. She wasted no time in making her way to the familiar old mansion.

Unable to enter the house without a key Nikki was forced to break the large bay window on the west side of the house. I'll have that fixed first thing tomorrow morning,' she promised herself as she entered the darkened house.

She fumbled around, easing her hands around the wall in search of a light switch. "You're here somewhere, damn it," she uttered in aggravation. An instant later, she flipped on the switch, but nothing happened. "Damn!" she cursed, but quickly remembered the emergency candles and where they were normally stored. Above the fireplace on the mantle in the large living room.

Nikki moved in the direction of the living room in an attempt to locate the mantle. "Finally," she groaned, after what seemed like an eternity.

Once a long stem match was lit, she spotted the three-pronged candelabra. "There, that's better." She sighed, quickly lighting the candles.

Most of the estate's furniture had been covered except for the wall paintings. She studied the portrait of her grandmother above the marbled mantle. The painting had always been one of Nikki's personal favorites. It was painted by French artist Pierre Deruet in the late thirties, when her grandmother Asia Alexandria Rourke was in her mid-twenties.

Nikki had inherited her grandmother's beauty, charm, and captivating smile. Asia Rourke had often whispered those words into her childish ears when she visited the estate. Nikki smiled at the memory of her grandmother.

Asia Rourke had been a strong-willed woman her entire life. She had been the backbone of the Rourke family. But her family's wealth had been squandered away by her own three children.

Nikki's father, Bradley Rourke had been a socialite with an appetite for gambling, women, and wine. A deadly combination as it later turned out. He fell to his death from a three-story apartment building in an attempt to sneak out of the bedroom window of a married woman because the young woman's husband returned home unexpectedly one morning.

Rumor had it that the woman's six-foot-two; two-hundred-fifty pound husband threw Bradley Rourke off the balcony in a fit of jealous rage. However, the husband and his wife left town several months later, never to be seen or heard from again.

Then there were Nikki's twin aunts, Aunt Belle Rourke Byrd and Aunt Sybil Rourke Casey. Both women lived wild, scandalous lives. Nikki's Aunt Belle died at the hands of her jealous younger third husband, and her Aunt Sybil passed away six-months later in a car accident, taking three other people to their graves along with her. Her aunt had been drinking heavily that day.

Such senseless tragedies, Nikki thought as she glanced at the oil paintings of the three Rourke siblings mounted on the east wall of the enormous living room.

To the left of the painting hung the portrait of Nikki's handsome grandfather Bradley Evans Rourke III, a fun loving man, much like his son. Bradley had died at a young age from food poisoning. His death had been ruled an accident, but as with any suspect circumstance resulting in someone's death, there had been rumors. Rumors ranging from Asia Bourke's hot temper, coupled with her occasional displays of uncontrollable rage, to rumors involving jealous husbands.

Nikki released another sigh of sadness as her gaze continued to travel around the room and stopped at her grandmother's extensive collection of French drawings from the fifteenth-century, etchings in chalk and watercolors. Jaques Callot's portrait of Claude Deruet, Pierre Mignard's, James II, and Jean-Antoine Gros's, Studies of Horses; Jacques Callet sketches of Ballet Dancers, Jacques Bellange's, The Three Mary's At The Tomb, Simon Vouet's Nude Women Playing A Lute, and Maurice-Quentin de La Tour's, self-portrait.

As Nikki continued her silent study of the etchings, she recalled word-for-word, her grandmother's explanation in detail to her as a child about the techniques used in fifteenth-century art. 'Some of these techniques Nikki are very ancient like the pen, brush, metal print, the black stone, sanquine, chalk, graphite (black-lead) and pastels. Nikki lovingly outlined the face on the self-portrait of Maurice-Quentin de La Tour while her grandmother's words echoed in her thoughts.

Nikki shook her head in an attempt to bring herself back to the present. She crossed the room and tried the switch on the table lamp, but it didn't work either. "Curses!" she mumbled. She picked up the candelabra and made her way through the kitchen into the utility room to the fuse box.

After changing the fuse, she crossed her fingers and made a silent wish before flipping on the main circuit breaker. Her wish was granted. An instant later, the lights were back on. "Thank God!" she exclaimed.

The huge house had been vacant for some time. Nikki had told her grandmother's long time servants, Bernice, their maid, and Alfred Posten their butler who also subbed as the Rourke family chauffer, gardener, and all around fix-it man, that they could live in the mansion for free, but Nikki could not afford to pay them. At first, the couple agreed, but two years later reconsidered and wanted to move back to Verona, Kentucky, to their hometown. That was nine months ago.

Nikki continued her journey through the house, making a mental list of everything inside. Amazingly, nothing seemed to be missing. Everything was in its place and working. That is, except for the rusty lock on the main entrance gate. Once again, she reminded herself to get the lock fixed first thing the next morning.

CHAPTER 14

"The Round Table," Tinker French said with slightly slurred speech. "The royal couple and their wedding party should dine at the round table."

Tipsier than the wedding coordinator for Gateau de Mers, the bride-to be Sidney Cox, hic-cupped as she nodded her agreement. She motioned for the waiter to bring them another bottle of red Bordeaux. "Yes, that sounds great. I'm sure Jill would love your idea, Ms. French," she finally managed.

"Thank you, Ms. Cox. I'm sure you're right. Ms. Gray would like my suggestion. Now, I think we're almost finished. Just a few more details. Are you up to it?" she asked.

Sidney downed her glass of red wine in one long swallow before responding. "Yes, I can manage," she said with a giggle. "Please call me Sidney and I'll call you Tinker. After all we have spent the biggest part of the day getting smashed together, I think we know each other well enough to..."

Tinker cut in. "Yes, of course. First names are fine. I've put a new tape in the recorder. Let's see," she said looking thoughtful. "Oh yes, the guest book. We'll place a large scroll and quill pen at the front entrance to the ballroom and assign actors the task of making sure the guests sign in. Good. Now all we need to do is discuss the entertainment and then the food." She smiled and picked up her drink.

Sidney nodded and poured another glass of red wine.

"We'll hire strolling court jesters, magicians, jugglers, minstrels, and of course, harp and mandolin players for the entertainment. Agreed?" Tinker asked as she refilled her glass.

Sidney nodded.

"Great! Now for the menu. Why don't we start with a raw bar? I'll have the chef hire an ice-carver to create something spectacular. Something to fit in the theme of things, of course. Maybe a castle, or perhaps King Author and Guinevere on horseback or something like that."

"Or maybe a huge clam or some other sea creature," Sidney offered.

Tinker frowned with distaste. "Umm, well, Sidney, sea creatures don't exactly go with the theme of things now, do they? Perhaps we should let the chef decide. Agreed?"

Sidney reluctantly nodded and downed another full glass of red Bordeaux.

"Now for the food items." Tinker said.

"Maybe you should check with her highness first!" Sidney snapped.

"Excuse me?"

"Sorry." Sidney filled her wine glass again.

"Mrs. Gray said for you to choose the foods you wanted, remember?"

"Why don't you do it, Tinker? You're the expert."

Tinker chuckled at the bride-to-be's drunken condition. "You know who you sounded like Sidney?"

"Her highness?"

"I was under the impression you and Mrs. Gray were the best of friends," Sidney forced a grin. "Oh, we are. Jill and I tease like that all the time."

"I can tell you've been around one another a long time. There for a moment..." Tinker paused to collect her thoughts, thinking to herself 'this could be juicy!' She leaned over to adjust the volume on the tape recorder brushing the side of Sidney's hand suggestively. She went on. "Friend's can be like that sometimes."

Sidney shrugged.

"How long have you and Mrs. Gray been friends?"

"Longer than I care to remember," she replied.

The surprised expression on the wedding coordinator's face was quickly concealed.

Realizing how she must have sounded, Sidney smiled. "We've been friends since high school. The ninth grade to be exact."

"Whew! That's a long time."

"Yes it is, isn't it?"

"Have you two always been close friends?"

"Not always."

"Really?" Tinker pried with growing interest, longing for something to gossip about with her, nosy friends concerning the billionaire's wife.

"Yeah, you know how it can be when you're a silly-ass teenager."

"Yes, it can be a trying, and confusing time, as I recall." Tinker replied, smiling and touching Sidney's hand again.

Sidney removed her hand from the table. "Yeah, one day you have a friend, and the next, that friend steals your boyfriend!"

"That sucks! I've had that happen to me a few times, too," Tinker said. "Friends can hurt you more than an enemy." She shook her head and lifted her drink.

Sidney took the empty wine bottle and waved it high over her head to attract the waiter's attention. "You can say that again sister!" she said.

A lot more conversation, another two hours, and several more bottles of wine shared equally between the bride-to-be and the wedding coordinator and the menu was finally completed. They were; at last, ready to stop for the day.

Clams, steamed mussels, oysters, and shrimp for the raw bar. Heart toasts with Salmon Roe Caviar and sour cream. Smoked Salmon with herb mayonnaise and cucumber sauce. Summer Beef Salad lined with Watercress. Lemon Chicken with sautéed lemon sauce, for the assorted array of hor'd oeavers. And the salads; Amienoise, a salad of Belgian, endives, apples, lettuce, and walnuts. And for the main meal, hearty Roast Beef, Roast Pig, Roast Lamb, Grilled Sword Fish on skewers, and Coconut Seviche on skewers, — Sidney passed on the hearty Meat Pies and Stews. The vegetables selected were; Haricots Blancs Sauce Picarde (roughly translated; dried white haricot beans simmered with onion and carrots topped with a thick onion sauce). Gratin de Choufleur Picarde (cauliflower topped with a thick onion sauce). Asperges a la' Normande (asparagus topped with cream). The bride-to-be's favorite. The soups selected were Soupe au Cresson Cauchoise, Cream of Watercress, and Potage Roscovite au Choufleur (cauliflower and potato soup). Fruit balls garnished with strawberries and assorted cheeses. The breads selected; carrot muffins, pumpkin muffins, cranberry and orange muffins, black bread, lemon poppy seed rolls, and yeast rolls. And for dessert, Amaretto cream pie, Grand Mandier cream pie, Old-English-Style bread pudding in vanilla sauce and of course, the wedding cake.

The bride's wedding cake was the only selection Sidney had made concerning her wedding. Sidney had been very adamant about the cake. Its shape would have to go along with the theme of things, that being a castle, of course. But the cake had to be baked by Ida Mae, a woman who was world renowned for her 'Cakes of Distinction.' She was a legend around Dallas. Sidney had seen her first Ida Mae Cake in the mid-eighties, at the wedding of her friend, Renee Braun. Ida Mae's Cake was amazing. Her Cakes of Distinction had graced the parties of Lady Bird Johnson, Robert Strause, Victoria Principal, and numerous other families of fame and high-society stature.

The wedding preparations were now completed. Tinker French knew she had her job cut out for her. All that was left for her to do was to hire a publicist and a photographer. This wedding was without a doubt not only going to be the social event of the year, but it was also going to be the wedding of the century as well. This event was going to make front-page headlines all over the world. She, Tinker French, would make sure of it!

C*HAPTER* **15**

Nikki Rourke wrapped a towel around her hair as she stepped out of the shower. And with a second towel snug around her body, she went in search of something to sleep in.

Her grandmother's nightgowns were too big. As were her twin aunt's. She did however manage to find a silk pajama top that once belonged to her mother, Elisabeth Theroux Rourke, a woman about whom she had mixed feelings.

When Nikki was thirteen her mother abandoned her, after the premature death of her father. Nikki was left with her mother's sister, Haley Theroux Callot who said her mother needed time alone to get her life back in proper working order. Her mother moved back to France and Nikki never heard from her again. That is until Nikki moved to France three years ago and hired a private investigator to find her.

The surprise reunion between mother and daughter was an emotional moment for both. Nikki's mother begged for forgiveness, something Nikki wasn't willing to give easily. The two women shared lunch, a little conversation, and Nikki went on her way, promising to stop by the theater house where her mother was performing to catch her show. But she still hadn't found time to do it.

Sitting on the side of the massive brass bed inside the bedroom once belonging to her mother, Elizabeth Theroux Rourke, Nikki continued to glance around the room. Memories she cherished of a woman she once idolized filled her thoughts. Night after night, she would curl up in the middle of her mother's king-size bed and study her every move. It became a nightly ritual. She loved watching the way her mother brushed her long, natural curly strawberry-blonde hair, one hundred strokes. She loved her mother's scent, so feminine, so pretty, so uniquely her.

Nikki remembered how mesmerized she had been by her mother's breathtaking beauty. 'God, how I wanted to grow up looking exactly like her.' Nikki sighed and rose to her feet. At her mother's dressing table, the tips of her fingers touched the priceless antique perfume and decanter bottles that were elegantly arranged on the table. She smiled and held some of her mother's favorites and read the labels. Guerlain in Paris, Pierre-Frances Paschal Guerlain 1828, Eau de Cologne Impe`riale, created for Empress Euge`nie 1853, Houbigant Perfume 1925, and La Belle Saison, The Beautiful Season.

"Oh, mother," she whispered, putting the perfume bottle that she had been studying back on the dressing table.

On her way out of the room, she glanced over her shoulder before closing the door.

She strode down the hallway in the direction of her father's room. Oddly, the door was open. 'Apparently an evening for memories,' Nikki thought entering the room. She flipped on the light switch, and noticed a favorite photograph of her father. "Daddy," she whispered, crossing the room and picking up the photo. She traced the outline of his handsome face with the tip of her finger, smiling as she recalled the moment in time the photograph had been taken. "Ah, such a happy day." She sighed and sat the photograph down. She switched off the light and pulled the door closed behind her, but just, as quickly, turned back when she heard a squeaking sound as the door swung open again.

Nikki popped her head back inside the room to check the latch on the door. It was broken. "I'll have that fixed tomorrow morning also," she whispered.

At the stairs, she sat down on the long mahogany banister railing and slid to the second floor landing as she had done as a small child. Some time between Nikki's fifth birthday and the present, the thrill of sliding down the banister had disappeared. "Damn!" She frowned as she tried to remove a small splinter from her shapely fanny. "Ouch!" she squealed as the tiny speck of wood slid out.

She made her way toward the patio smiling as she remembered it was her favorite place to play as a child. Nikki opened the glass doors, hurried outside, and walked up to the railing to survey the estate grounds.

Nikki's grandmother had spent most of her time at Rourke Manor in the saltwater farmland along the southern shoreline of Long Island.

Rourke Manor was originally purchased to become the family's summer mansion. To Asia Rourke, however, it felt more like home. So as it turned out summer, winter, spring or fall, didn't matter. Asia Rourke enjoyed the quiet, yet gracious, country mood of Rourke Manor year round.

The enormous grounds invited ease and relaxation. The grand manor's pillared porches and spacious rooms evoked a comfortable feeling of the South.

Rourke Manor was partially hidden behind tall hedges as were most Victorian Mansions built in the early 1900's by Stanly Stewart, the brilliant bon vivant architect, whose designs were favored by the elite of New York and Newport.

Romantic elements came in abundance at Rourke Manor with tall white Corinthian columns and fanlight entrance. The structure boasted a high roofline with dormers, a closed hexagonal porch to the side, and behind, a sweeping deck and open columned porch.

The landscape at the rear of the house was amazing. Adjacent to a long lawn, was a tennis court, pool, and guesthouse.

The acreage was generous, but not massive, pleasurable, but not pretentious. To the south of the house was a second floor balcony with a spectacular view of the enormous pond once home to feisty swans and ducks.

Nikki had made many wishes looking at a sky filled with shooting stars. She had sweet childhood memories of Rourke Manor. She smiled, glancing at the pond as she recalled watching the ducks taking their morning baths and the delightful afternoons of enjoying tea with her grandmother.

"Oh, Grammy, I miss you so much," she said. She shook herself free from her memories and started back inside. Then it hit her like a ton of bricks. She remembered her friend Gabrielle. "Oh my God, Gabby," she cried running into the house.

In an instant, Nikki was dressed. She dashed out of the house to search for the nearest working telephone.

CHAPTER 16

The traffic moved along the freeway faster than Corbin Douglas could have hoped for. A short time later, the taxi carrying his lady of mystery pulled into the entrance gate of a massive mansion bearing the name of 'Gray' boldly etched across the rod iron gate.

"Son-of-a-bitch! That red hair. I should've known," Corbin mumbled. He drove his car at a turtle's pace past the mansion.

He parked across the street from his client's home trying to decide whether he wanted to go inside and have a little chat with the billionaire. He needed answers to the ever-growing number of questions he had. He pulled up to the entrance gate, and pressed the intercom.

As the P.I. was being ushered to his client's study by the butler, he overheard Forrest Gray shouting at the woman who had just entered the house. Corbin caught a glimpse of the couple as he strode past the living room.

The butler opened the door to Forrest Gray's study and motioned Corbin inside. "Would you care for something to drink while you wait for Mr. Gray, sir?" Corbin crossed the room and sat down in a chair. "No thanks," he replied, glancing at his watch.

"Mr. Gray will be with you momentarily, sir," Scottsdale said, pulling the door closed behind him.

Corbin glanced at his watch again, and then jumped to his feet, as his gaze zeroed in on a 1914 Babe Ruth rookie card, minor league, Baltimore Orioles. On the reverse side of the card was the at home and abroad schedule of the famous baseball team. "Cool," he whispered, and picked up the case-mounted card for a closer look. He shook his head with envy and put the card back in its proper place. He continued to glance around the billionaire's amazing study, with its priceless antiques, memorabilia and, pieces of artwork.

A pair of Muhammad Ali's boxing trunk's, shoes, and the robe the famous boxer had worn on the day of his bout with George Foreman in Kinshasa, Zaire

1974 securely cased and mounted on the opposite wall of the room, caught his roving gaze. The robe was an amazing collector's item, to be sure. It proudly showed a silk handkerchief stitched to its lining with an astrological prediction of the fight's outcome. Corbin read the impressive facts card inside the glass case that explained the out come of the boxing match on that day.

He didn't hear Forrest Gray enter the room.

"A gift from my wife," Forrest said, striding past the private detective on his way to his desk.

Corbin turned to face the billionaire. "Whew! You have some pretty remark-able things in here."

Forrest shook his head and gave a gesturing wave of his hand around the room. "All my wife's doing, I assure you," he said, pulling out his chair to sit down.

"You sound annoyed," Corbin said, sitting in the chair opposite his client.

"Really?" Forrest replied in a questioning voice. "Hmm, — well, I didn't mean to."

"I'm sorry to intrude Forrest, but..."

The billionaire cut in. "But you'd like some answers." he said, leveling his gaze on the detective.

"I have no idea where to begin." Corbin shrugged.

The billionaire closed the study door. "Okay, I'll go first," he said, glancing over his shoulder at the P.I.

"Shoot," Corbin returned.

"I phoned Nikki in London last night," Forrest said. "It was rather late. She was at the apartment I have been renting for her for the past two years. She was still very upset about the young woman who had been shot at the airport a week earlier there." Forrest pulled out his chair and sat down.

"Ms. Villano," Corbin said, meeting Forrest's eyes. "Camellia Villano. That was her name wasn't it?"

"Well, well. You have been working, haven't you?" The billionaire smiled.

"The corner of Corbin's lips twitched as he fought back a grin. " That's what you hired me for."

"Not exactly, Detective. I hired you to keep an eye on Ms. Rourke when she arrived in New York. But when Nikki wasn't on the flight I booked her on, I then asked you to find her."

"That's what I've been trying to do."

"What?"

"Locate Ms. Rourke."

"I don't understand."

"You want to cut the bullshit?" Corbin snapped, jumping to his feet.

"Meaning what, Detective?" Forrest returned, motioning for the P.I. to sit back down.

"You know as well as I do that Camellia Villano, Rachel Ward, and Gabrielle Graves' murders are somehow connected. At the very least you must surely…"

Forrest interrupted the private investigator in mid-sentence. "Oh yes. Another murder. Ms. Graves. That is amazing. Two murders on the same day. I heard about Ms. Graves' murder late this afternoon. Pity," he said, shaking his head.

"Can we get back to the conversation that you had with Ms. Rourke last night? I need to know what she told you. It might help me track her down," Corbin said.

Forrest shrugged. "Not much to tell, Detective. Nikki was still upset over her friend's murder a week earlier. She told me that at the last minute she had asked Camellia to sub for her as something came up and she couldn't make it. Camellia needed the extra cash and jumped at the offer. Later that evening, Nikki found out that her friend had been murdered at the airport."

"The same way Ms. Ward was asked to fill in for her last night, at the last minute."

The billionaire nodded. "Apparently."

Corbin sighed. "So Ms. Rourke was afraid to go to the airport?"

Forrest nodded. "Yes. I told her not to worry about it, that her imagination was getting the better of her. I promised that, I would make the flight arrangements myself. And would hire someone to meet her at the airport and make sure she boarded the flight safely."

"And who did you hire?" Corbin asked with growing interest.

"Well… no one. I thought Nikki was being ridiculous. I wanted to prove to her that…"

"What?"

"Calm down, Detective. At the time, I thought Nikki was over-reacting." Forrest shrugged.

Corbin jumped to his feet again. "Her friend was murdered as she waited for a flight just a week earlier, and you thought she was over-reacting?"

The billionaire motioned for the P.I. to be seated again. "I know what you're thinking. You think Camellia was shot instead of Nikki."

Corbin sat back down. "And you don't?" he asked with surprise.

"Not at first anyway. But now…"

Corbin cut in. "But now that two more of her look-a-like friends have been murdered…"

"That's right Detective. At first I thought Camellia may have been murdered because of who her father is and his jaded past…"

"His ties with the Mob," Corbin said knowingly.

"That's right."

"Okay, I can buy that, for the time being anyway, but if that was the case with Ms. Villano then why were Ms. Ward and Ms. Graves murdered? And where is Ms. Rourke?"

"I don't know why Rachel and Gabrielle were murdered or where Nikki is. I can't believe she hasn't contacted me. Surely she knows I'm worried sick."

"And you're sure she hasn't tried to contact you?"

The billionaire shook his head. "She hasn't, and I'm worried about her. Maybe you should go to London..."

Corbin interrupted. "No. I'm not ready to go to London yet." Corbin shook his head. "Did Nikki, I mean Ms. Rourke know about Mr. Villano's former connections with the Mob?"

"I have no idea. If Nikki knew, she didn't mention it to me." The billionaire rose and went to the wet bar. He poured himself a shot of brandy and offered Corbin a drink.

"No thanks," Corbin said. "You know, Forrest, it really is remarkable just how much Ms. Rourke, Ms. Villano, Ms. Ward and Ms. Graves look alike. Amazing. Did you date all four women?"

A stunned expression crossed the billionaire's face. He swiftly regained control, and cleared his throat. "Is that what you think, Detective?"

"I'm just trying to..."

Forrest cut in. "The answer to your question is yes. They were all dear to me in their own way. But do you think that has anything to do with these murders?"

"What do you think?"

"I think none of this has a goddamn thing to do with finding Nikki," Forrest returned, going to the bar and pouring himself another shot of brandy. "Are you sure you wouldn't care to join me Detective?" he offered, waving the brandy bottle in midair.

"No thanks," Corbin said, as he watched the billionaire return to his chair. "Do you think Ms. Rourke is in New York?"

"I don't know. Like I said, she hasn't tried to contact me. The last time we talked to one another was last night. But then I've already told you that."

"I believe Ms. Rourke is in danger." Corbin's voice held concern.

Forrest nodded in agreement. "Me too. You have to find her Corbin," he said before belting down his shot of brandy.

"Did you book the hotel suite at the St. Regis for her?"

"Yes, certainly."

"Did you know Ms. Graves signed into the hotel under Ms. Rourke's name?"

"No, of course not."

"Was the woman who came into the house just before me, Mrs. Gray?"

The billionaire stood, walked to the bar again. He poured himself another shot of brandy and then leaned against the railing as he sipped the drink. "My wife. Yes, that was Jill, why?"

"I couldn't help overhearing part of an argument you two were having."

"Sorry about that Detective."

"Does Ms. Rourke have any family in New York?" Corbin asked.

Forrest sat his glass on the bar. "Sadly, most of Nikki's family has passed away."

"Including Ms. Rourke's mother?"

"Ah, Nikki's mother. No, actually, her mother is alive and well. And she is performing on stage somewhere in London."

"She's a dancer?"

"No, she's an actress. But not a very good one," Forrest said taking his drink back to his desk.

"Were Ms. Rourke and her mother close?"

"No. Nikki's mother abandoned her when she was thirteen years old. An aunt raised her, I believe."

"And what about Ms. Rourke's father?"

"He's dead. Fell out of some young married woman's bedroom window a long time ago, or so I was told."

"Where did Ms. Rourke stay when she lived in New York?"

"With her grandmother, Asia Rourke. Her grandmother died about three years ago."

"And that was the last time Ms. Rourke was in New York?"

"I think so."

"Where did her grandmother live?"

"Long Island. The Rourke Manor Estate, in Quogue."

"Is there anything else you can…?"

The P.I. was silenced when his client's wife entered the room wearing a sexy negligee and matching silk robe.

"Oh, darling! I'm sorry, I didn't know you still had company," she said, as she drew closer to her husband.

Forrest stood, pulled his wife to him and kissed her cheek. "That's all right, Jill. Say hello to Mr. Douglas. Corbin, this is my lovely wife, Jill Jefferies Gray," he said with a smile.

Corbin offered his hand and smiled as their gaze met. "Mrs. Gray."

"Mr. Douglas. How very nice to meet you," she said, as she continued to study his face. "You look rather familiar. Have we met before?"

"Not formally. But I think we may have run into one another earlier this afternoon." Corbin smiled.

"Oh really? And where might that have been Mr. Douglas?" Her voice held surprise.

"In an elevator at The St. Regis Hotel," Corbin said.

Jill Jefferies Gray shook her head and smiled. "No, I'm afraid not. I was in town today, but I was at The Waldorf Astoria. I had an extremely long lunch with a friend. We're in the middle of planning her wedding, and then I stopped at Sotheby's."

Corbin noticed his client's expression had changed from happy to angry. Then Forrest released his arms from around his wife's waist and said, "Well Corbin is there anything else I can…"

"I should be running along," Corbin said. He turned to leave, giving a nod to the billionaire's wife.

"Oh, Mr. Douglas," Jill said, stopping Corbin before he reached the door. He turned.

"Mr. Douglas, I just remembered where I saw you. It was today. You were at Sotheby's. You bought a fisherman's lure box."

Corbin smiled. "Yes, that's right. I guess that must be where I saw you." He turned to leave, but the billionaire stopped him.

"Just a minute Corbin, I'll walk you to the door," he said. "I'll be right back Jill," he added, leaving the room with the private detective.

On their way down the long corridor heading for the front door, Corbin said, "You certainly have an incredible home, Forrest," His gaze continued to scan the elaborately furnished billionaire's home.

"Thank you, but I personally think it's beginning to look a little too… what's the word I'm looking for," he paused, searching for the correct words. "Ah yes! Over crowded. My home is starting to look more and more like a goddamn auction house rather than a home." He shook his head in dismay.

"Your wife's hobby?" Corbin asked.

"Jill can't refuse," Forrest smiled as he glanced at Corbin.

Corbin nodded. "I know what you mean about your wife's spending habits. She had a blast at Sotheby's. Mind boggling, actually," he said with a chuckle.

The billionaire halted. "Just curious, mind you Detective, but how much did Jill spend this afternoon. Do you recall?"

Corbin shrugged. "You sure you want to know?" he asked, making a cringing face.

Forrest nodded. "Ball Park?"

"Roughly thee maybe four," he replied as he watched his client's expression change from anger to relief.

"Thousand? That's not bad for Jill."

Corbin cleared his throat. "Ah no. Actually you need to add a few more zero's to that number, I'm afraid," Corbin said, as he watched the expression on his client's face turn to rage.

It took several moments for Forrest to regain his composure. " My wife. She's really something isn't she? Her one true passion in life seems to be her never-ending efforts to drive me to the poor house."

Corbin sensed the billionaire's attempt to amuse was made for his benefit, but deep inside Corbin also knew Forrest Gray was upset with his wife.

"Women," Corbin returned not knowing what else to say. "Good night,

Forrest. We'll talk tomorrow," he added, as Scottsdale opened the door for him to exit.

Forrest went to the bar in the living room and poured himself a double shot of brandy, and turned his attention to the butler. "Scottsdale, have Chapin bring my Mercedes around front, "he said. " Tell him I'll drive myself tonight, and then tell Mrs. Gray not to wait up for me. Something came up, and I have to leave for awhile."

CHAPTER 17

'Oh my God, will this nightmare ever end?' Nikki Rourke thought, as she thanked a nearby neighbor for the use of a telephone. Nikki's call had been to The St. Regis Hotel. She wanted to check on her friend, Gabrielle Graves, and make sure she had signed in okay, and to warn her to be careful, especially after the morning shooting at the airport where another one of their friend's had been shot and killed.

Nikki had told Gabrielle the night before that she could stay at the posh hotel under her name, since Nikki no longer needed the room. But Nikki changed her mind and decided to come to New York incognito at the last minute.

She wanted to surprise Gabrielle with her visit and share the room with her after all. But after the morning shooting at the airport Nikki became terrified and disappeared forgetting about her friend until a short time ago.

After being told over the telephone by a hotel employee the shocking news of her friend's murder Nikki felt faint and needed to sit down. She asked permission to use the neighbor's phone a second time. With trembling fingers, Nikki dialed the number that was handed to her, as she sat down on the chair next to the telephone and, tried to collect her thoughts.

Nikki's second telephone number was for a taxi. Then her grandmother's friendly neighbors invited her to join them for a little conversation and a hot cup of tea while she waited for her ride to the ferry.

Trying desperately to hide the fear building inside with each passing moment, Nikki knew when to respond, when to smile, and when not to, even though she didn't remember what had actually been said to her during their polite conversation.

The taxi driver dropped her off at Saks Fifth Avenue, where she charged an expensive new outfit, matching shoes, handbag, and a honey-blonde, shoulder-length wig.

An hour later, Nikki had another taxi driver drop her off at a nightclub where she hoped her former boyfriend still worked tending bar. "Please be there, Kyle," Nikki whispered, as she entered the dimly lit Blues Club.

Nikki pushed her way to the bar and claimed the only empty barstool in the busy club, spotting her former boyfriend immediately. She breathed a sigh of relief and sat waiting to see how long it would take Kyle to recognize her in her disguise.

The Blue Gibson was in full swing, its usual norm for that time of the evening. Nikki ordered a shot of tequila with a wedge of lemon from one of the other bartenders working behind the bar. She was on her third shot of tequila before Kyle finally recognized her. He stood speechless for a few moments as he continued to stare at Nikki in total disbelief before approaching her.

"Oh, my God. It is you. I don't fucking believe it!"

Nikki smiled. "It's me," she returned, as she reached for her drink.

"We gotta talk, Nikki," he said, leaning over the bar to kiss her cheek. "You're in serious danger, love. I've been trying to track you down," he added in a whisper.

"I know. I need your help, Kyle. I don't have anyone else I can turn to."

Kyle nodded. "Sure Nikki. You gonna stay here at the club and wait for me to get off tonight?"

She shrugged. "I have nowhere else to go." She sighed again. "Guess I'll have to hang around here," she added, belting her shot of tequila and then sucking on the wedge of lemon.

"Great," Kyle said, and his face suddenly lit up. "You can do me a favor," he said, with a grin.

Suspecting what her former boyfriend had in mind, she shook her head. "No way! I don't feel like sitting in tonight, Kyle."

The bartender smiled that ever-so sexy smile of his that no woman in her right mind could resist. "Please Nikki," he said, with a playful pout.

Nikki gave in. "Oh, all right. But only one song. It's been awhile and I'm out of practice."

Kyle chuckled. "You, out of practice? Give me a break. You're the best goddamn Blues Singer in New York, Nikki." He reached for the bottle of tequila and poured her a shot.

"I haven't sung a note in almost three years. And I seriously doubt if I can remember the words to any of the songs anymore," she countered, reaching for the shot of tequila.

"Listen babe. When it comes to singing and you, it will sort of be like riding a horse – once you're back on top, hey…you know what I'm trying to say?"

"Umm," Nikki mumbled.

"I'll take a break in a few minutes okay? Go on back to the dressing room and pick out a gown. Oh, and by the way, you look hot as a blonde."

"I thought you were a red haired woman kind of guy," she responded.

"Hey babe, you'd even look great bald," he said, with a wink.

Nikki giggled. "Bald? Are kidding?"

Kyle chuckled, as he picked up the bottle of tequila and poured Nikki another shot. "Take this with you. I'll be back in a few minutes." He handed Nikki the shot glass.

The Blue Gibson was a typical Blues Club. The dimly lit smoke-filled club was a popular nightspot for blues lovers of all age and class groups.

Kyle and Nikki met and fell in love there almost five years earlier. Nikki had been a singer at the Blues Club before she became friends with Jacqueline Collins. Nikki reminded the famous dancer of herself at Nikki's age. Not long after their meeting, they became friends, and Jacqueline convinced Nikki to move to France and go to work for her as a well-paid exotic dancer. Nikki's decision to move to France caused her and Kyle's breakup.

Kyle never got over his love for Nikki. Soon after she left for France, he began drinking heavily and dating many women. Most of them were married, and extremely wealthy, willing to give the handsome young bartender anything he wanted as long as he continued to supply them with sex. The three-letter word that makes the world go round.

On Kyle's way to the dressing room to join Nikki, he stopped at the pay phone to make a quick telephone call.

"Hey baby. Sorry to wake you…" He paused after he realized the voice on the other end of the phone wasn't the voice he had expected. "Who the fuck is this?" he snapped into the receiver.

"You want Sidney? Hold on while I wake her," The masculine female voice said before laying the receiver down.

"What the fuck?" Kyle mumbled, as he strained to hear what was being said.

"Sidney. Wake up babe it's for you. Some jackass with a hard on wants to talk to you," the person on the other end of the wire slurred, causing Kyle to chuckle.

Kyle could feel himself growing aroused as he listened to the soft moans of passion being played out in his ear by the two intoxicated women.

"Oh, Tinker that feels so good. Lower, please. Lower," Kyle recognized the voice of his friend, and suddenly found himself wishing he could be in the mix of it with them.

"Damn," he groaned, putting the phone down. He spent the next few moments attempting to calm himself before joining Nikki Rourke in the singer's dressing room.

Hearing the door open Nikki glanced over her shoulder. "Oh, Kyle, you scared the hell out of me. What took so long?" she said, as he entered the room and closed the door behind him.

"Sorry babe, I had to make a pit stop, Hey, you look fabulous! Good enough to eat, actually," he said, as he rushed across the floor and pulled her into his arms.

Nikki pushed him away. "Please don't Kyle. Not now," she said, inching away a few steps.

He pulled her back into his arms. "God, how I've missed you, Nikki," he said in a low, hurt whisper.

"I know Kyle, but we need to talk." She looked at him with a frightened expression. "Someone is trying to kill me."

"Yeah, I know," he responded.

A look of confusion crossed Nikki's face. "You know? How could you possibly know something like that?"

Kyle threw his hands up in the air and shook his head. "Some rich broad I date once in awhile told me."

Nikki's mouth flew open in stunned disbelief. "What?"

Kyle took Nikki by the hand and escorted her to a chair. "Sit down. It's a long story."

Nikki sat down and tilted her head to look at him.

"I started dating some broad a few months ago," he said. "She's the best friend of…" he stopped talking when one of the female singers walked into the room. He turned his attention back to Nikki and winked. "We'll finish this later. You're up next."

"But…"

Kyle silenced Nikki with a kiss. "We'll discuss this later," he whispered.

Nikki turned her attention to the mirror behind her. She gave herself a quick once over before leaving the dressing room to make her way to the stage.

CHAPTER 18

Between the web of colored Italian flags that canopy the streets for about a three block radius between Mulberry and Canal in Little Italy sits Milano's, an Italian restaurant owned by Frank Milano. A restaurant where Internationally known Milanese Chef Paul Lombarida's nightly specials not only keeps Mobster Figure Carmine "Blade" Asaro coming back night after night, but it also keeps the five man F.B.I. undercover surveillance team coming back night after night as well.

Chef Lombarida, Internationally famous for his 'Ossibuchi' (a veal braised in a herbed white wine and tomato sauce) his "Risotto" (hearty rice dish in which rice is simmered in broth with butter, Parmesan Cheese, and saffron) and his "Bollito Misto (a boiled mixed meat dish in a rich sauce). Carmine's personal favorite...that and Chef Lombarida internationally famous "Panettone" (a buttery yeast cake studded with raisins and candied fruits) for dessert.

"Buona sera, Mr. Asaro."

"Good evening, Frankie. I'll take my usual table," Carmine said, as he strode past the Italian restaurant owner.

"Naturalmente, signore." ("Of course, sir.")

"Just have the waiter bring me the chef's special tonight. Capisce?"

"Capisce. Un bicchiere di Chianti, signore?" ("I understand. A glass of Chianti, sir?)

Carmine glanced back over his shoulder at the restaurant owner and nodded. "Bottiglia Chianti, Frankie." ("Bottle of Chianti, Frankie.")

"Si signore." ("Yes sir.")

As Carmine strutted through the popular restaurant, he glanced around his surroundings, spotting a couple of familiar faces sitting at the bar, Joey Mezzogiorno and Eddie 'Styles' Costa. The two men were the top two 'Movers and Fixers' for The Juliano Crime Family.

Unknown to Anthony Juliano, both Joey Mezzogiorno and Eddie 'Styles'

65

Costa were part of a covert F.B.I. sting operation that had been secretly placed inside the Juliano Organization. Their job was to get enough evidence to put the organization out of business.

"Hey you two, come join me and the guys," Carmine shouted at the two men sitting at the bar laughing and joking together.

Both men glanced over their shoulder at the man with the familiar voice. "Hey Carmine," Joey called out, standing up and sliding his barstool back. "We'll be right there," he added, reaching for his wallet and pulling out a ten-dollar bill. He tossed it on the bar. "Keep the change, Vinnie," he said, with a wink to the bartender who was also an undercover F.B.I. agent.

Moments later, Joey and Eddie sat down at the table with the three mobsters Carmine, Donnie and Vito, who were sharing stories about their individual day's work and laughing at one another's misfortunes, trails, and tribulations.

With his mouth still crammed full of food, Carmine interrupted Eddie's story of the day. "You guys think you had a bad day? You ain't heard nothing yet," he said, reaching for his glass of wine.

The two F.B.I. agents shared a quick glance. "What Carmine? You think you had a rougher day than me and Eddie here?" Joey returned, waving his hands in midair.

Carmine nodded and swallowed his bite of food. "Yeah that's right, I did. At least you two guys weren't sent to whack some broad. God, I hate that! Especially when the broad is good-looking." He reached for his glass of wine.

"What are you talking about, Carmine? You know me and Eddie ain't in that end of the family's business. We're in the money end," Joey said. He shook his head. "You guys always get to do the fun stuff. Don't they Eddie?" Joey glanced at his friend, and picked up the bottle of Chianti.

"Fun stuff?" Carmine spat, and shook his head in aggravation. He swallowed another mouthful of food. "Fun stuff my ass, Joey. It's hard as hell whacking a classy broad like the one we was supposed to hit this morning. Anyway, as it turns out somebody beat us to it. Pissed Mr. Juliano off big time."

"What? What the fuck you talking about Carmine?" Joey asked.

Carmine picked up the cloth napkin, wiped the grease from around his mouth, and then tossed the napkin onto his empty plate. "No shit! This was the craziest damn day. Swear to god, you guys." He belched and then went on. "Mr. Juliano gave the order to me, Donnie, and Vito this morning. ' Go to the airport, he says. Meet the flight in from France. There's this redhead on it. The only redheaded babe on the flight. Pop the broad the minute she steps off the flight. Then get the fuck out of there.' Just as I get the broad in my goddamn sights, from out of nowhere 'BAM' somebody beat me to it. Can you fucking believe that shit?" Carmine shook his head, picked up his glass of wine, and downed it in one long swallow before continuing. "And are you ready for this shit?"

Vito cut in. "Carmine thinks it was another broad that popped the redhead."

"Shut the fuck up, Vito. I was telling the goddamn story," Carmine snapped. He shook his head. "Where the fuck was I?" He reached for the bottle of wine. "Never mind. I remember. As it turns out the broad who got popped was the wrong broad. Boy was Mr. Juliano pissed!" Carmine shook his head.

"No shit? What did Mr. Juliano say?" Joey asked, sneaking a quick glance at his partner sitting across the table from him.

"What part of pissed off don't you understand, Joey? I'm telling you the boss was hotter than hot, he was smoking!"

"So what happened next, Carmine?" Eddie asked.

"Don't ask me how he found out so fast, cause I don't know, but Mr. Juliano phones me. Tells me to have my ass ready in ten minutes. The bitch he wanted popped just checked into the St. Regis, so…" Carmine paused for a sip of his drink.

"What, Carmine? Shit, spit it out, you're killing us here!" Eddie exclaimed.

"Keep your dick in your pants Eddie. I'm getting there," Carmine barked. "Me and Mr. Juliano are sitting inside his limo watching for this broad to come back to the hotel. The guy at the desk told us she checked in and then went right back out. So we're just sitting there waiting for her to return. Suddenly, I spot the bitch come bouncing down the street. So, I jump out of the limo and wave to Donnie and Vito. They jump out of their car and we go inside the hotel. By the time I make the bastard at the desk tell me which room this broad is staying in…" Carmine paused to light a cigarette. "You guys just ain't going to believe this one…swear to god," he said, shaking his head at the memory. "The fucking broad was already dead. Honest to god, someone beat me to it. Pop! Right in the back of the goddamn head. I'm telling you the bitch has some pretty heavy enemies." Carmine shook his head and motioned for the waiter to bring them another bottle of Chianti.

"Jesus, Carmine! What did Mr. Juliano say then?" Joey asked, as his gaze followed the waiter approaching their table carrying a telephone in his hands.

"Excuse me, Mr. Asaro. A telephone call for you, sir." The waiter, wearing a tag with the name of Neko on it, handed the phone to the mobster. Joey shot Eddie a quick glance.

Carmine nodded to the waiter and accepted the phone. "Yeah? Oh, Mr. Juliano. Yeah. Shit! I don't fucking believe this shit! Where was she spotted? Okay, I'll take care of it Mr. Juliano. Calm down. The broad won't see the light of another day. You can take that to the bank, sir!"

Carmine handed the telephone back to the waiter. "Shit," he spat. "That was the boss. We gotta go. Come on Donnie, Vito. We gotta track that goddamn broad down. Somebody spotted the bitch getting out of a taxi in front of Sax Fifth Avenue. The bitch at the St. Regis, guess what? Another goddamn wrong broad," he said, shaking his head in dismay.

Joey watched as Carmine jumped to his feet. "No shit, Carmine, you are having a bad day. You guy's win hands down over me and Eddie's bad day."

Carmine leveled his cold eyes on the federal agent. "Yeah, and if we don't find that goddamn broad soon it might be me, Donnie, and Vito that wind up sleeping with the fishes. We'll see ya guys," Carmine said, as he motioned for Donnie and Vito to follow him.

Joey glanced across the room at a man and woman sitting at a small table beside the restaurant's front window. He nodded. The lady returned the gesture. A split second later, the two federal agents posing as a couple left the restaurant.

Chapter 19

Corbin Douglas reached for his cell phone as he slid into his car and started the engine. "Not enough hours in the day sometimes," he mumbled, as he dialed the telephone number of the New York City Police Department. Moments later, the P.I. was talking to his friend, Charlie Miller.

He told him about the conversation he had earlier in the day with Jacqueline Collins regarding Anthony Juliano and his theory about the Mobster's possible involvement with the three young dancers.

Forty-five minutes later, the P.I. was sitting at the bar inside The Scarlet Ribbon drinking Chivas on the rocks and chatting with his former crime-solving partner.

"Used to be gangsters were merely errand boys for the politicians and gamblers. They were at the bottom of a highly stratified milieu. The gamblers were under the politicians who were 'kings.'" Miller paused to light his cigarette and then went on. "Of course, that all changed with prohibition. Prohibition turned gangs into empires. He released a puff of cloudy smoke. "Then came the syndication of organized crime turning the power structure upside down."

Corbin shook his head and picked up his drink. "Is there a point to your history lesson, Charlie?"

The two men shared a glance. "Who was it that once said, 'there is something sacred about big business,' Corbin?"

Corbin chuckled at his friend. "What? A pop quiz so soon in the school year, Charlie," he returned smiling. "I believe it was Henry Ford, Icon of the American Capitalist Spirit and notorious Anti-Semite. How did I do professor?" he said, as he motioned for the bartender to bring them another round of drinks.

"Very good, Detective. I'm impressed!"

"Yeah, yeah, yeah. Like I said before Charlie, your point?"

"After our phone conversation about Anthony Juliano, I phoned my brother Brill."

Corbin cocked a curious eyebrow. "And?"

Charlie chuckled, as he reached inside his jacket pocket and pulled out a note pad. He opened it and began reading. "At eleven o'clock a.m. arrived home after quick meeting with two attorneys. Kramer Davenport and..."

Corbin cut in. "No shit? Kramer Davenport. I knew that son-of-a-bitch was a piece of slime!"

"What?"

"Davenport, that piece of shit. He's Regina's ex."

"No shit?"

"Yeah, no shit. Go ahead Charlie, sorry I interrupted you," Corbin said, suddenly curious as to where his girlfriend might be after he remembered the flowers her ex had sent to her office earlier in the day. He shook the thought from his mind, and turned his attention back to the homicide detective.

"All right," Charlie replied, and began reading from his note pad again. "At eleven o'clock a.m. arrived home after quick meeting with two attorneys. Kramer Davenport and Paul Cucchiara. Three men were already inside Juliano's home waiting for him to return. One of the men inside Juliano's study had been arrested the night before on a D.U.I charge and wanted Juliano to put a call in to the judge that he has on his payroll, and ...well, you get the picture."

Corbin nodded, understanding what his friend meant. "Go on, Charlie what else did Brill give you?"

Charlie glanced at his note pad. "Another one of the men in Juliano's study asked Juliano to put a hit on his girlfriend for cheating on him, and the third guy was in from Chicago looking for work."

"So what does all this have to do with the three young dancers deaths, Charlie?" Corbin asked, as his gaze scanned the elaborately run nightspot for men.

"Juliano was followed to The St. Regis Hotel by my brother and a few other F.B.I. agents early this afternoon."

"What? Then, why don't you go and arrest his ass?"

Charlie shook his head. "Can't! Brill said Gabrielle Graves was all ready dead by the time Juliano's hit squad got there. A woman matching the description of your client's wife was seen in the hotel about the same time, though."

"Yeah, I rode up on the elevator with her, I think. Whoever the mystery woman was got on at the seventh floor."

"Then it couldn't have been the same woman you saw?"

"Not necessarily."

"What do you mean?"

"Maybe this woman (if the killer was in fact a woman) suddenly remembered she had left something at the murder scene, something that could incriminate her, and so she decides to go back and..."

"I see your point. Maybe Madam 'X' didn't expect the body would be discovered so quickly. So she stops in her tracks, takes the fire stairs to the seventh floor, and then presses the elevator to take her back up. Makes sense."

"The woman I was on the elevator with was very upset, after seeing cops all over the place as she stepped off the elevator. She damn near ran me over trying to get back on. But, as far as our Madam 'X' being my client's wife, I couldn't say with any certainty, Charlie."

"You met Mrs. Gray tonight?"

"Yeah sure, but I couldn't swear in a court of law that the woman in the elevator was…"

"Well, why the hell not? You got a look at both women."

"Well, not exactly. The woman in the elevator was wearing a huge, floppy hat and designer sunglasses. I didn't even notice the color of her hair. She was a babe all right though." Corbin shook his head.

"Do you remember anything at all about her?"

"When she first got on the elevator she was on her cell phone to some guy."

"Do you remember if she mentioned this guy's name?"

Corbin looked thoughtful for a moment. "No, not really."

"How about the conversation she was having? Can you remember any of that?"

"Oh, shit Charlie! I've had one hell of a day, and I think I may have given new meaning to the phrase 'agony of defeat,'" he mused, shaking his head.

Charlie glanced at his watch. "Want to go up the street to this Blues joint I know of and have a night cap with me?"

Corbin smiled. "Some broad you like works there?"

Charlie could feel his face flush. "Yeah, well we've talked a few times."

"What about Bette?"

"Ah hell, Corbin, you of all people know how hard it is to keep a relationship going in our line of work." Charlie shrugged.

"I know how much you loved Bette."

"I think it was more like lust, amigo," Charlie said, in a teasing manner.

Corbin sat his empty drink glass down. "What's the name of this Blues Club?"

"The Blue Gibson. Ever heard of it?"

Corbin shook his head and shifted on his barstool. An instant later, he glanced at the homicide detective. "Wait a minute, Charlie," the P.I. exclaimed. "I think that might have been the name of the club the woman on the elevator mentioned to the person she was talking to on her cell phone." He paused thoughtfully and then said, "Kyle. Yes, I think that was the name I overheard her call the person on the other end of the phone line. I'm sure of it, Charlie."

"Do you remember anything else?"

"She said the word geeze a few times, and then she went on to say all right, already. If I have to bring her there myself, she'll be there. And then she said the name of the club, The Blue Gibson."

"Guess what?" Charlie grinned.

"They have a redheaded barmaid?"

Charlie chuckled. "They have a bartender named Kyle."

"What does he look like?"

"Young, late twenties, well-built, give or take; about six-foot, hazel-colored eyes, curly hair to his shoulders, sandy-blonde, I think. Why?"

"I think you just described the man I saw leaving The St. Regis Hotel earlier this afternoon."

"What kind of car was he driving?" Charlie asked.

"He slid inside a stretch limo and seemed to disappear into thin air."

"He had a driver waiting for him?"

Corbin shook his head. "No. This guy was the driver. I wish I could drive in this goddamn city like that kid. Amazing." His tone was one of envy. "Why?"

"I think our man Kyle drives a forest green Mustang."

"Really?"

"The kid's father works for, are you ready for this?" Charlie smiled.

"Forrest Gray?"

"Good guess, amigo!"

"So now we can place my client's wife, Juliano's hit squad, and the son of Gray's butler at the St. Regis Hotel around the time of Ms. Grave's murder."

"And perhaps even the billionaire himself."

"So, what does it all mean?"

"Well, we have a billionaire, and his wife, their chauffeur's son; the billionaire's missing mistress, three dead dancers, a gangster and his hit squad. Somehow it's all connected but the question remains, how?"

"Indeed."

"You're not going to believe who just strolled in." He nodded in the direction of the six-foot tall billionaire being ushered to a table closer to the stage.

Corbin stood up and pushed his barstool out of the way.

Charlie looked at his friend. "You going over to say hello?"

Corbin shook his head. "No, I've had enough of this place."

Charlie stood, but someone seated at the corner table caught his roving eye. "Check out the table in the corner to my right, Corbin. You know who that is?"

"You mean the ugly guy with one of Juliano's goon's growing out the side of his neck?" Corbin asked.

"That's Juliano's high-priced attorney, Paul Cucchiara."

"You mean consier (counselor), don't you?"

"I think today's crime lord's consier likes to be referred to as counselor."

"You ready to go down the street for that nightcap?"

"Might as well. There's enough undercover agents in this place tonight to start our own government."

"Nothing's going to go down in here tonight anyway, Charlie."

"How do you know?"

"Well, for one thing, Nikki Rourke isn't here."

"I see your point. That is to say if Nikki Rourke has been the real mark all along."

"Who else could it be?"

"Maybe all three young dancers were someone's target all along."

"Umm, that's an interesting theory."

CHAPTER 20

Homicide Detective Charlie Miller was a handsome man. Midnight black hair with the slightest hint of gray starting at the temples. Dark mustache and romantic almond-colored eyes. Towering over most people at a respectable six-foot-three inches. Muscular build. A man who enjoyed working out and taking good care of his body. Of course, in his line of work taking care of one's body was mandatory.

"Momento senor, por favor," The cocktail server said to the homicide detective as Charlie Miller crossed the room heading for the nearest empty table.

Charlie glanced over his shoulder and shrugged at his friend, P.I. Corbin Douglas. "I guess he wants us to wait while he cleans off a table."

"No problem Charlie," Corbin said, and glanced around the dimly lit, smoke filled nightclub. "Sure is hazy in here, don't you think?" he added shaking his head.

"I think that's how most blues clubs are, amigo." Charlie smiled.

"Yeah maybe, but the smoke in this place is a little much," Corbin struggled with a cough.

"It's been awhile since you've been to a blues joint hey, amigo?" Charlie asked with a chuckle.

Corbin nodded. "Ah yeah. Guess you could say that, Charlie. Counting this time it's my first." He smiled. "So sue me."

"No kidding! Your first time?"

Corbin shrugged. "Why? Does it show or something?

Charlie smiled. "No, of course not. The thick smoke is part of the lounge act. Ambience, they call it. It clears out after the show. It isn't really smoke per se it's dry ice. See the machine up on stage?" Charlie pointed in the direction of the stage.

Corbin's gaze followed Charlie's gesture. He spotted the female singer. "Check out the singer. What a body," he gasped. "Hey Charlie, ask the waiter to see if he has a table closer to the stage, will you?"

"Oh, so you do like the club after all, hey amigo?"

Corbin laughed. "Well, at least the singer got my attention. Who is she?"

"I don't know. I don't think I've seen her in here before. And believe me with a body like that I would have remembered."

Corbin followed his friend to the table.

While Charlie ordered drinks, Corbin stared at the beautiful young singer. Unexpectedly, he found himself attracted to her and her incredible emerald-green eyes.

"Oh my god, Charlie. I think I've died and gone to heaven," he said as he continued to stare, delighted that the young woman seemed equally attracted to him when she openly returned Corbin's attention.

"Yeah, I can see that, amigo," Charlie said as he lifted his drink.

The female singer was a real heart stopper. The private investigator, lost in thought, knew he had never met her before yet there was something oddly familiar about her...her eyes...the way they sparkled as she looked at him. The way the lights shadowed around her smile. "Oh, god, that smile. She has the most amazing smi..." Corbin stopped speaking and the expression on his face changed from lust to disbelief.

Charlie studied his friend's stunned expression. "What the hell is wrong with you, Corbin?"

The P.I. was too stunned to answer.

Nikki Rourke could feel the P.I.'s eyes watching her, undressing her. Her eyes, her smile. 'Oh, my god! The look on his face is that of a person who has just recognized someone they haven't seen for a while.' Nikki thought as she witnessed Corbin's expression change from turned on to turned off in ten seconds flat. Nikki fought the impulse to jump off stage and dodge out the back door of the club. An instant later, she handed the mike to the piano player whispered in his ear, and then she vanished.

The piano player made a gesture to the stagehand and he released another puff of smoke from the dry-ice machine filling the room with a huge cloud of smoke.

"Corbin, for Christ sakes will you say something. What the hell is wrong with you?" Charlie asked.

Corbin jumped to his feet and motioned for his friend. "The smile. Come on Charlie let's go back stage. The singer." He paused. "That's her!" he shouted, raising his voice over the loud applause.

"Who? What?" Charlie asked, jumping to his feet.

"Nikki Rourke! The singer is Nikki Rourke, Charlie. I'd know that smile anywhere."

Charlie grabbed his friend's upper arm. "Are you sure? The broad that was just singing had blonde hair."

Corbin turned to face the homicide detective. "Haven't you heard of wigs? Shit! She must be trying to hide. Come on before she leaves the club."

By the time the two men made it backstage the beautiful blues singer had disappeared.

"Son-of-a-bitch!" Corbin shouted, realizing Nikki Rourke had vanished into thin air right before his eyes.

Charlie shrugged his broad shoulders with uncertainty. "What now, amigo?"

"I don't know. Maybe I'll ask around outside. Charlie why don't you start with Pretty Boy Floyd behind the bar?"

"Who?" Charlie asked scratching his head as Corbin walked toward the nearest fire exit.

"The bartender. Kyle," Corbin shouted over the noise as he shoved the fire door open. Moments later, the P.I. was outside asking everyone he passed if they had seen a beautiful blonde leaving the club and if so what direction she had taken. Detective Charlie Miller stayed inside the club asking questions about the blonde-haired woman that was on stage. Starting with the bartender.

The P.I. got lucky. The fourth person he stopped said she noticed a woman running from the back entrance of the club in the direction of the bus stop. She also noticed that the woman in question was being followed by a couple of goons in a black shiny Cadillac.

Corbin followed the bus he believed Nikki Rourke to be on. He stayed out of sight as it dropped people off at the ferry heading to Long Island. Apparently, Nikki Rourke was going to her grandmother's estate in Quoque. 'She must've been hiding there all along.' Corbin thought as he pulled his car into a parking lot adjacent to the ferryboat.

Corbin hopped on the ferry just as it was ready to take off. He kept a respectable distance from Nikki not wanting to spook the long-legged beauty. Corbin also kept his distance from Juliano's three goons.

After the ferry docked, Nikki Rourke managed to ditch Juliano's three goons before making her way back to her grandmother's estate. Corbin found himself admiring her cleverness. Luckily, however, Nikki never spotted him. A few moments after Nikki entered her grandmother's estate Corbin quietly followed.

It was getting late. The air was damp and cool and carried the salty scent of the Atlantic. Even so, Nikki found it refreshing. She inhaled deeply as she opened her bedroom window.

After she showered, Nikki went back to the kitchen and made herself a pot of black rum tea. Sometime between stepping off the ferry and stepping out of a hot shower, Nikki decided what she had to do. She was tired of worrying about what a new tomorrow may or may not bring for her. She went back to her bedroom and began to tape record the past three years of her life. Nikki hoped that telling all into the tape machine would help her figure out who wanted her dead. And if at the end of her taping she still had no answers then the tapes might help someone solve her own murder. Nikki sighed, comforted by her newfound sense of strength.

CHAPTER 21

"Listen you guys. That bitch is out there somewhere. And before sunrise, we gotta find her, capisce? I don't give a fuck if we have to do a house by house search around this place, Anthony wants that broad found and permanently silenced!" Carmine shouted at the other two thugs standing beside him.

One of the young thugs with Carmine gave a nervous sigh of dread. "Carmine, look around this place. There must be at least a hundred houses. There's only three of us. What are you talking?" he said, shaking his head in total disbelief.

The mob figure grabbed the young thug up by the collar of his shirt before lighting into him. He leveled his cold gaze on the goon. "The bitch is in one of these houses hiding. I don't give a fuck!" Carmine released the guy from his powerful grip and shook his head.

The other thug jumped into the conversation. "I don't know, Carmine."

Carmine gave his friend a dagger-like glare. "Who gives a fuck, Donnie? Now you two guys stop giving me a hard time, get the lead out of your ass, and help me find that goddamn broad!" he barked and nodded in the direction to the right. "Vito you go that way and Donnie you take off to the left. I'll go back down to the ferry and wait around in case the bitch tries to get back on. Oh, and fellas if either one of you guys see that goddamn, nosy private dick, shoot him in the back of his goddamn head too, I hate that son-of-a-bitch!" He sighed shaking his head. "Did you guys see how smooth he thought he was on the ferry? I can't believe that stupid dick actually thought we didn't spot his sorry ass."

Vito chuckled. "Yeah, that's right, Carmine. After all, you'd recognize that prick in your sleep. How many times did he bust your ass when he was a cop? Ten, fifteen maybe."

"Hey, fuck you, Vito!"

"Calm down, Carmine. I was just pulling your chain. I didn't mean nothing by it." Vito said.

"Yeah, well you should be more careful Vito. You don't want to put me in the goddamn mood to have to yank your chain, capisce? Now you and Donnie get your sorry asses going and don't come back down here until after you finish that goddamn broad. I'll go and phone Anthony to see if he might have an address on her family or something. And while I'm at it, I'll have him send in a few more guys. Now get out of here!" he said. He began walking in the direction of the flashing neon sign ahead advertising the twenty-four-seven coffee shop.

*****

After being stood up for the third time in a week by her boyfriend, Regina Prescott made a decision to give Corbin Douglas a taste of his own medicine. Determined not to be home if he stopped by, she agreed to have dinner with her former lover, Kramer Davenport.

Regina glanced at her watch with a heavy sigh. "It's getting late Kramer. Maybe I should forget about having that nightcap you offered at Kelsey's and..."

The attorney smiled as he interrupted her. "I don't think so." He pulled Regina suggestively into his arms and kissed her.

"Umm," she moaned and slowly melted.

"God, I miss you, Regina," Kramer whispered in her ear as his warm breath sent goose bumps up her spine.

"What do you want from me, Kramer?" she groaned, pulling free from his tight embrace and fumbling inside her handbag for the set of keys to her car.

"What do you think?" he asked, stopping her clumsy attempt to locate her keys. "Please, Regina. You had too much wine at dinner. You're in no condition to drive home. I'm taking you to my apartment," he said, putting his arms around her shoulders and guiding her away from her car into the direction of his parked car.

"But..." she offered in quiet protest, remembering how wonderful his lips had felt a few moments ago. She glanced up at him and swallowed. "Please," she whispered objecting.

He silenced her with a passionate kiss. "Umm, please, huh? Is that a request, baby?" he whispered in playful jest across the side of her throat with his warm breath, again causing her to shiver.

"Oh, Kramer," she whispered in surrender as he began to unbutton her silk blouse. The evening air felt refreshing on her skin.

Kramer lowered his head, kissing Regina's neck and right shoulder, making his way to her full round breasts, while his left hand was busy unfastening her pink, satin lace bra from behind. An instant later, he was kissing, licking, and sucking first one breast and then the other, causing her to moan with eager anticipation.

"I can't wait to get home, Regina. I want to make love to you now," he said bringing his mouth up to meet hers.

Unable to speak, Regina placed his hand on her right breast in surrender.

Thirty minutes later, the hot-natured attorney exploded his heated release for the second time deep inside the female attorney in the back seat of the company owned Town Car. A car that in reality was owned by underworld figure, Anthony Juliano.

*****

The grand opening of the Scarlet Ribbon had been a tremendous success. Jacqueline Collins released a silent sigh of gratitude while she continued to exchange goodnight kisses with the few remaining customers as they left her club. She caught a glimpse of high-powered attorney, Paul Cucchiara, motioning for her to join him at his table inside the lounge area. She nodded and released herself from New York's Senator Al Florention's embrace. She crossed the lounge floor to join the attorney who worked for Anthony Juliano.

"Some place you have here, Jacqueline," he said, gesturing around the club with a wave of his hand.

"Thank you, Paul. I'm glad you approve."

"Top of the line. Just like you," he said, gesturing for her to join him in the booth.

"I'd love to," she said, smiling.

"Anthony sent me. Says for me to tell you thanks for the tip on the Rourke broad. He would have never known Camellia had told her anything if it hadn't been for you. He wants you to know that he owes you."

The famous dancer smiled. "It was nothing. After all the favors, he's done for me in the past. I figured it was me that owed him. Especially after he made Edward stay away from me like he did. There would be no Scarlet Ribbon if it had not been for Anthony."

"Anthony is a good friend."

Jacqueline nodded in agreement. "Has he found Nikki yet?"

"I don't know." He shrugged. "But if he hasn't, you know Anthony. He will."

The club owner nodded. "I'm surprised Nikki hasn't phoned me, especially after Gabrielle's ..." she stopped talking after noticing one of the bartenders paying more attention to what she had been saying than he should have been.

The high-powered attorney glanced at her and followed her gaze. Without speaking, he nodded to the thug sitting opposite him before turning his attention back to the beautiful club owner.

"Well Jacqueline, it's getting late. Guess we'd better roll. I'll telephone you tomorrow," he said, gesturing for Jacqueline to get out of the booth so he could. He kissed her on the cheek. A few minutes later he was sliding into his parked car outside the club, and the goon that had been growing out the side of his neck earlier in the evening was hiding in the shadows lying in wait for the nosy bartender, Dillon, to walk out of the elaborately run nightspot for men.

CHAPTER 22

"'A glimpse of perfection!' Is what Jacqueline Collins said to me in her attempt to let me know just how much in love with Forrest Gray she still was: Jacqueline smiled as she continued to gaze into my eyes. She went on. 'You know Nikki, it was love at first sight for me, and of course, it was lust at first sight for Forrest. But that didn't matter to me. I mean, his caring less for me than I cared for him. I just knew somehow if I gave Forrest what he wanted, you know, make it real good, better than he'd ever had it before sexually'... Jacqueline stopped talking then and her expression changed to a sad one. She swallowed and then started talking again. 'I knew that I could win his love, take him away from her...his wife I mean'." Nikki paused, and poured herself another cup of black rum tea before speaking into the tape recorder again.

"I remember the sadness I felt for Jacqueline as she continued to explain how her affair with Forrest Gray had begun. ' He took me to visit China on our first trip away together. We stayed at the Grand Hyatt Hong Kong. Our hotel suite was absolutely magical'. She sighed and closed her eyes as she remembered her time with Forrest. It was as if the scenes from their heated past were being played out in her mind. She continued to talk. 'Nikki have you ever stayed somewhere, where the surroundings were to die for?'

"I had never known anyone that much in love before. Jacqueline started talking again. 'The hotel we were staying in had a terrace overlooking the ocean. The sky seemed to melt into the sand and the sight was so breathtaking it seemed to melt into me. Nikki, it was literally a feeling of divineness.' She then turned to face the window in her office."

Nikki paused briefly to put the tape recorder down and change the tape in it. After changing the tape, she spoke into the mike again. "Tape number three," she said, and then glanced at the clock on her nightstand "Let's see. Where was I?" She paused for a moment to reflect. "Oh, yes. I remember," she said. " Jacqueline walked to the window in her office and began to stare out of it as she continued to confide in me. ' For the next six months I was in heaven', she sighed. 'I stopped seeing Edward Stacy III all together. And because of it, Edward was not a happy camper'. She shook her head at the memory. 'Edward wouldn't leave me alone. Nikki, the man actually threatened to have me killed if I didn't come back to him,' she said, and turned to look at me. I remember my mouth flew open in stunned disbelief at Jacqueline's shocking words. I asked her what she did about Edward's threat and her response was surprising and maybe even a little troubling too." Nikki swallowed as the memory flashed inside her mind.

She went on. "Jacqueline laughed and turned away from the window to face me again. It was an evil laugh. Her expression rapidly changed from a solemn one to one of hatred and her eye color just as quickly changed from her normal color of emerald-green to a sinister shade of black. The transformation was disturbing. All I could think about after that was finding an excuse to leave her office. 'Gee, look at the time'. I remember saying in an attempt to bring Jacqueline's state of mind back to the present. But she ignored me. 'Men!' Jacqueline snapped. 'They're all bastards'. Jacqueline leveled her eyes coldly to mine. It made my skin crawl. Jacqueline walked closer to me after her outburst and brushed a loose strand of hair out of my eyes. I remember stepping back from her touch."

Nikki paused and turned off the tape recorder when she heard a noise coming from outside. She rose and walked over to the bay window inside her bedroom and glanced out. The leaves on the century old trees were gently swaying back and forth. The millions of shining stars were twinkling brightly in the sky and the moon was full. A typical spring evening at Rourke Manor, she thought. Nikki sighed and continued to glance around the estate grounds.

Not noticing anything out of the ordinary, Nikki dismissed the sounds she had heard. "Just my nerves," she mumbled, and made her way back to her bed, changed the tape, and picked up the small microphone again. "Tape four," she said, and then cleared her throat.

Nikki went on to talk in detail about the on again off again romance between Jacqueline Collins and Forrest Gray. The billionaire's fascination with beautiful redheads was apparently his one true weakness in life. "Camellia Villano, Rachel Ward, and Gabrielle Graves. Jacqueline was upset when she discovered that Forrest had been sleeping with Camellia, Rachel, and Gabrielle behind her back."

"Soon after each affair the dancers, one-by-one, left the club managed at the time by Jacqueline. Strangely, the three young dancers and Jacqueline remained friends. Now that I think about it, Jacqueline was actually the one who found top-notch modeling assignments for Camellia, Rachel, and Gabriele, as well as for myself." Nikki sighed.

"A week ago, Camellia stopped by my apartment in London. She told me that she wanted to leave town for a while. She said she was frightened because she had overheard a conversation that she shouldn't have. When I questioned her she said it would be better if I didn't know." She paused.

"Camellia knew that I was leaving for New York the following morning. I was going to do a photo shoot for The House of Duvall's summer catalog. Camellia asked me if she could come along. Instead, I turned the assignment over to her. It was obvious to me that Camellia needed to get away for a while. I phoned Pierre to okay the last minute change."

"That was the last time I saw Camellia alive. I found out later she had been shot and killed at the airport. I was devastated. At first, I thought Camellia must have been killed because of the conversation she overheard. I tried to phone Forrest but he was out of town. At least that's what I was told when I phoned his office. I asked his secretary where he had gone, hoping he was going to surprise me with an unexpected visit. I really needed to see him at that point. Anyway, I was told that his secretary wasn't at liberty to say." Nikki stopped and took a sip of her tea.

"After I found out about the shooting, I went over to Camellia's family's house, but I was turned away at the door. Her father told me that it would be best if I'd just stayed away. When I asked him what was going on, he shut the door in my face. So out of despair I telephoned Jacqueline at her London penthouse and asked if she would have lunch with me the following day. She was in town trying to drum up new customers for the grand opening of her new nightclub in New York. The following afternoon we met for lunch and she asked me if I would do her a favor and help her out for a few weeks. How could I refuse? After all, she was the one who jump-started my career and because of her, I've become one of the highest paid dancers and models in France. I could have never made it on my own."

"If I didn't love Forrest so much, I would feel guilty for having a relationship with him behind her back. Jacqueline has never found out about Forrest and me. It would kill her if she knew. She still thinks Forrest will eventually divorce his wife and marry her." Nikki shook her head.

"At lunch that day, Jacqueline told me that Forrest was the reason she had decided to open The Scarlet Ribbon in New York instead of London. She wanted to be closer to him. I never had the nerve to tell her that Forrest didn't love her. He never had. He felt sorry for her. He said it was tough on Jacqueline to have once been young, beautiful, and desirable, and then wake up one morning and find that her hay-days had ended, over, caput. Even in middle age she was still trying to hold onto her youth...a nip here, a tuck there, wigs in place of what once was a beautiful thick head of hair. 'How sad', he said, as he continued to talk about the former French playmate turned dancer. 'Poor Jacqueline'," he said. 'Nikki, I think Jacqueline is losing it. Do you know what she tried to tell me on more than one occasion'?" She cleared her throat and went on.

The Shadow of Her Smile

"I remember smiling and shaking my head as I went to the bar to freshen our drinks. ' She has been trying to convince me that my wife has paid her several visits. Threatening visits demanding that she stay away from me.' Forrest laughed as though he were amused at such a ridiculous thought." Nikki paused and took a sip of her tea.

Forest continued, "I told her, 'Jill asked you to stay away from me? That is the most ridiculous thing I have ever heard in my life.' I just couldn't imagine it.' His tone took on an edge. The sharpness bothered me. "Nikki sat her teacup back down.

'Jill doesn't give a shit what I do, or for that matter who I do it with. All Jill gives a shit about is my money, how she can spend it, and how quickly she can drive me to the goddamn poor house.' He laughed again before belting the remainder of his drink." Nikki yawned, and then continued to talk into the microphone.

"Forrest said, 'Nikki, I'm telling you. Jacqueline has become a thorn in my ass. I don't know what I'm going to do with her. And to tell you the truth, it's starting to worry me', he said, as he stood up and walked to the bar to pour himself another shot of brandy. I followed him and as he picked up the bottle of brandy, I put my arms around his waist and laid my head on his shoulder. 'Why don't you talk to her? Just be honest with her, Forrest. Tell her you aren't in love with her and be done with it.' I suggested. But he laughed at me, sat the liquor bottle down, and then pulled me around to face him. His laugh was one of amusement. It made me feel childish and stupid." Nikki reached for her cup of tea again.

"Forrest complained, 'You can't talk to a woman like Jacqueline once she gets her hooks into you.' He paused. 'You go to great pains to keep a woman like Jacqueline from...' He stopped talking and shook his head. He pulled me into his arms. 'Nikki, I want you to stay away from Jacqueline. She's trouble. Take my word for it; I know what I'm talking about. She knows people, some rather serious people. And she knows how to use them to get what she wants.'

"What are you talking about?' I asked him. Forrest released me, walked over to the patio, opened the sliding glass door, and went out onto the terrace. I followed. When I tried to question him further he silenced me with a kiss. We made love and he left the next morning. He told me he had to go back home before his wife spent all his money." Nikki turned off the tape recorder, stood up, yawned, stretched, and then walked out onto the terrace to get some fresh air. The view wasn't as pretty as the view from the second floor terrace so she decided to go and make herself another pot of hot tea, take the tapes and the tape recorder with her, and finish the taping session from the second floor terrace. She was determined to get the tapes finished before morning. If Nikki really was in danger, she wanted to leave clues as to who might want her dead.

After Nikki sat her cup of tea down on the patio table beside the shoebox that now contained fourteen tape recordings and the small tape recorder, she pulled out the recorder and shoved in a new tape. "Tape fifteen. Right after Camellia's death, I began to ask myself some painful questions. Questions about my relationship with a married man. It is painful falling in love with a married man. At first it seems harmless enough, then things become complicated, they spin out of control. What to do? You either learn to accept the way things are and face it, or walk away. Yes, there are many decisions to make, I told myself. Is being in love with a married man fair? To me? To his wife? To him? He was a man who would always belong to his wife. Jill Jefferies Gray. Forrest loves her. Completely. Without regret. He loves her. So why all the other women? Why me? Who knows?" Nikki shrugged. "I either have to accept it or walk away. I must admit, I wish I could walk away from him. Start over. But who am I kidding? I love him too much and I'm not that strong. Is it because of Forrest that somebody wants me dead? Could it be Forrest that wants me dead? Has he grown tired of me? He knew I would be arriving in New York this morning." Nikki looked thoughtful for a moment and then went on.

"Could it be Jacqueline who wants me dead? Could she have found out about my relationship with Forrest? Oh, god! That's an eerie thought, but the facts suggest that it's possible. Forrest did have affairs with Camellia, Rachel, and Gabrielle, and now all three dancers are dead. Jacqueline knew I'd be arriving in New York this morning from London and she also knew I'd be staying at the St. Regis for the next two weeks." Nikki shivered as she tried to figure out who it was that wanted her dead.

"Maybe it's Forrest's wife. Maybe Mrs. Jefferies hired someone to knock off her husband's mistresses. Get us all out of the picture and be done with it," she said. "Oh, that's silly. Forrest has been having affairs behind Mrs. Jefferies back since they've been married. And knowing Forrest as well as I do there will always be more women." She shrugged.

"Of course, there is another option I've yet to consider. Camellia's visit to me the night before she was murdered. She told me about the conversation that she overheard. A conversation that she shouldn't have listened to. I suppose Camellia could have been followed that night. Maybe someone thinks Camellia told me about that conversation. Maybe the conversation was so important that the parties involved didn't want to take any chances. Maybe they think I'm a loose end..." Nikki stopped talking and cleared her throat. "Stop it Nikki! This is ridiculous. You're making yourself crazy. If that were true then whomever killed Camellia would have killed both of us that night inside my apartment." She paused to reflect. "No, I don't think so. Now what, Nikki? You're back to square one again. Back to the person linking you, Camellia, Rachel, and Gabrielle, which is Forrest Gray. Could I actually be in love with a man that wants me dead? It's sad, isn't it? It is almost as ridiculous as me pointing my finger at Jacqueline for heaven sakes. Jacqueline has made me who I am today." Nikki sighed.

After hearing a strange noise, Nikki instinctively stopped recording and shoved the tape player inside the shoebox with the tape recordings she had spent the biggest part of the evening making. She jumped to her feet and leaned over the large cast-iron skirt-hooping of the terrace.

The silhouette of a person was lying on the ground beside the pond illuminated by the full moon.

"Oh, my god," she whispered and slowly backed against the outside wall of the mansion. Too terrified for rational thought, Nikki stood frozen against the cold wall shaking violently in the shadows, trying as best she could to avoid the light from the moon.

Moments later, she heard someone running up the steps inside the house

CHAPTER 23

What seemed like an eternity of cowering in the shadows against the cool wall of the terrace Nikki Rourke finally felt that it was safe enough to come out of hiding. In reality it had been an hour since she heard the front door to her grandmother's home slam shut behind the intruders as they left the estate. She glanced at the patio table and was relieved to see the shoebox containing the tape recording still there.

Nikki was now certain it was herself that had been the intended target for a murder. No more skirting around it, someone wanted her dead. Nikki collapsed into the cast-iron patio chair, placed her shaking hands over her face, and let her tears fall.

Before the break-in, Nikki had thought someone wanted her murdered. There had not been any real facts or evidence for her groundless suspicions and theories. Now, someone had broken into her grandmother's home. The truth was terrifying. It was suddenly a cold, hard fact. If the intruders had found her, she would have been murdered. She would not be sitting on her grandmother's patio trying to figure things out. She was back to square one.

Nikki wiped the tears from her blurry eyes and opened the shoebox. She stared at the fifteen tape recordings. Who could hate her enough to kill her?

Nikki felt she had done a good job dodging the three goons who had followed her from the Jazz Club. So how did they know where to find her so quickly? Sure, Forrest Gray had known about Nikki's family home, but that was a long time ago, and even though she had told him about her childhood at Rourke Manor, she had never actually mentioned the estate's address. And with no phone service inside her grandmother's home there would be no need for the phone company to list the address of the estate in their local directory. But yet out of nowhere... BANG! There they were. Men who had been sent to murder her. Nikki continued to try and sort things out in her confused mind.

Suddenly, she saw the face of her former boyfriend. "Kyle," she whispered his name softly, remembering he had been to Rourke Manor many times in the past. But Kyle also knew the estate had been put up for sale eight months earlier, so why would he or anyone else for that matter, even consider the idea that she would be hiding out there? "No, Nikki, that idea is ludicrous. Not in a million years would Kyle do anything to hurt you," she mumbled and dismissed the notion. It couldn't be Kyle. It had to be Forrest, Jill Jefferies Gray, or Jacqueline. Why would Forrest want her dead? All he would have to do is tell her it was over. Unless he was targeting his wife and having all his look-alike lovers knocked off first to take suspicion away from himself and send it into the direction of a madman on the loose—a madman that had a thing for redheads. Yeah, that could be it. Oh, my lord! Is it possible? 'Yes, Nikki, that theory does sound plausible.'

Maybe Jill Jefferies Gray found out about her husbands many affairs with women resembling herself and out of spite, or perhaps revenge, she ordered a hit on all of them. She is the one person who would have the most to lose if Forrest decided to leave her for someone else. I have little doubt that the divorce would not only be front-page headlines but it would be a very costly and nasty divorce. Another strong possibility, to be sure. That is to say unless Mrs. Gray signed a prenup. Hum. Nikki considered the possibilities as she drummed her fingernails on the cast-iron table.

Suddenly, the image of the man she had noticed lying on the ground before the break-in leaped into her thoughts. "Oh, my god!" she exclaimed, jumping to her feet and rushing to the brass skirting on the patio. She leaned forward and saw a man lying on the ground beside the pond.

Nikki ran down the long flight of stairs and straight through the kitchen toward the back door. With a great deal of dread, she jerked the door open and rushed down the pathway to the pond. Her heart seemed to be beating as fast as her feet were running. The air was damp and cool and carried the salty scent of the nearby saltwater farmland along the southern Atlantic shoreline.

Under the brightly lit full moon, Nikki spotted the man lying near the pond. She cautiously approached him. She recognized him as the man she had been flirting with at The Blue Gibson. She released a sigh of uncertainty. She wanted to help him, but she was afraid he might be one of the men sent to kill her. Nikki sat down on the ground beside him, thinking he must have slipped, lost his footing, and somehow hit his head.

She lifted his head onto her lap cringing at the bloody sight. She should go for help, but she was too afraid. Not certain if he was alive, she finally managed enough nerve to check and see. Unable to feel his pulse at his neck with her fingertips, Nikki raised his head up and slowly placed it back down on the cold, damp ground. She shifted her position, unbuttoned his shirt, and put her head against his chest. His heartbeat seemed normal enough…slow and steady against her ear. "Thank god!" she mumbled.

Nikki's gaze studied the handsome stranger's features, his broad shoulders, muscular arms, manly chest, narrow waist; lean hips and strong masculine legs. Definitely a man who takes good care of the body, she thought, shifting her gaze back to his face. She studied his lips, high cheekbones, defined brow, and thick, dark-brown hair. Nikki was having difficulty imagining this man as a pay-for-hire killer.

How could she get him into the house?

As though he heard her thoughts, he moaned. Still half-dazed he attempted to sit up. Somehow, Nikki managed to get the stranger onto his feet and into the house. Getting him to wobble up three flights of stairs was difficult but somehow, she managed to guide him to her father's bed. The stranger collapsed again into an exhausted sleep.

Nikki removed his wet clothing, his gun, and an 8X10 yellow envelope from his jacket and pulled the top sheet up and over his shivering, naked body. She left the room. A short time later, she returned with a warm pan of water, soap, towel, washcloth, and a first aid kit.

After dressing his wounds, Nikki took the stranger's wet dirty clothes to try and clean them as best she could. On her second trip up the long flight of steps, she carried with her a pot of hot black rum tea, hoping the injured man might manage a cup if he should wake up.

Several hours dragged by. Nikki dozed in the rocking chair her father had rocked her to sleep in when she was a small child.

It was dawn before she opened her eyes. She stretched, yawned, and jumped to her feet, remembering the night before. She crossed the room to check on the stranger in her father's bed.

He didn't seem to have a temperature. His heart was beating normally, and he appeared to be sleeping. She pulled the sheet back up to cover his shoulders and tiptoed out of the room. She closed the door only to stop a few moments later when it popped open again. "Damn!" she muttered, reminding herself to have the door lock repaired as soon as possible.

CHAPTER 24

Corbin opened his eyes with a great deal of effort. "Jesus!" he complained when the pain from his head injury forced him to close his eyes again. His hand flew up to touch the painful area. "Son-of-a-bitch!" he mumbled, feeling the bandage wrapped around his head. Corbin lowered his hand and gazed around the room. "Where am I?" he whispered, forcing himself to sit up. He studied his surroundings unable to recognize a thing. He attempted to get out of bed, and as he did so, the sheet fell to the floor. It almost tripped him in his clumsy attempt to rise to his feet.

"Shit!" he spat, wobbling over to the closet. He closed the closet door as quickly as he had opened it. The strong fumes of mothballs held him at bay. "Whew!"

Corbin staggered across the room to the antique dresser, hoping he would have better luck with the items neatly tucked inside the drawers. He found a pair of flannel boxer shorts, picked them up, shook them out, and put them on. The shorts were two sizes too big, but he left them on anyway, more anxious to try to figure out where he was, and why he was there. Leaving the room, he saw the long spiral staircase and slowly began the painful descent. The spectacular view of the century old trees and large pond from the second floor terrace caught his attention. He couldn't resist the scenic view as he walked out onto the terrace.

Glancing over the skirting of the terrace, he saw a young woman jogging along the pathway leading to the pond. She was wearing a yellow cotton t-shirt with the neckline cut out. It was tied with a knot at her curvy mid-section, and she too had on a pair of flannel boxer shorts several sizes too large.

Corbin continued to log the young woman in his mind. He wondered who she was, and why he was there with her. Height about five-six. Hair, long, and red, pulled back into a ponytail. Light skin suggesting she preferred to get her exercise in before the sun became too hot. Corbin cleared his throat. "Good morning," he shouted. Nikki Rourke stopped and turned.

She put her hands on her shapely hips and breathed harder than she meant to. She was afraid, but tried not to show it. She leaned her head to one side and raised her index finger as she continued to gasp for breath. "I'll be right up." She was panting loudly but she forced a small grin as she continued to try and catch her breath.

Soon, Nikki made her way upstairs carrying a tray with two teacups and a pot of black rum tea. 'I'm en route to join the man that may have been sent here to kill me and I'm offering him a civilized cup of tea before my demise.' Nikki thought as she joined the stranger on the terrace.

"Good morning," he said

Nikki cleared her throat and set the tray on the cast-iron table. "I hope you like tea. I'm afraid that's all I have in the house right now." She glanced at him. "How do you feel?" she asked pouring them both a cup of tea.

Corbin cringed. "I feel like shit! If you really want to know the truth about it."

"I see," Nikki said. "Well, to tell you the truth, with a head injury like that," she pointed to his bandages. "I'm surprised to see you out of bed at all."

"What happened?"

Nikki shrugged. "I'm not sure."

Corbin's eyes widened with interest. "I don't understand. What do you mean you don't know what happened to me?"

Nikki sat her teacup down and shrugged. "I have no idea what happened to you last night. I don't know who you are, what you want, or why you're even here. This is my grandmother's house and..."

Corbin interrupted looking surprised. "What? You don't know who I am?"

"I was sitting out on the terrace last night when I saw you lying on the ground by the pond. I went down to check on you and ..."

Corbin cut in again. "You don't know my name?"

"I have no idea who you are or why you were on my grandmother's property."

Corbin shook his pounding head. "I don't know who I am or why I'm here either."

"Drink up. You should force yourself to have something."

Corbin's gaze studied Nikki's smile. There was something familiar about her incredibly sexy smile. He lifted his cup and took a small sip. "Mmm, this is good. What kind of tea is it?"

"Black rum. I like flavored teas. Do you?" She returned his smile.

He chuckled in spite of his pain. "I'm not sure," he said.

Nikki pointed to Corbin's bandages. "Your head injury is pretty serious. Of course, I'm no doctor, but I did the best I could." Her tone was apologetic. "I'm not very good at that sort of thing."

Corbin put his cup down. "Why didn't you take me to a hospital?"

Nikki sighed, "I didn't have any way to get you there. I don't have a car here or a telephone, and the closest neighbor is almost four miles away. And it was very late…"

Corbin stopped Nikki from finishing. "Hey, it's okay. I should probably be thanking you for taking care of me instead of asking you all these questions." He picked up his teacup again.

Nikki shifted her gaze away from him as she searched for something to say. Food, she thought, realizing Corbin must surely be hungry. "Are you hungry?" Her tone was one of concern.

He chuckled, "Now that you've mentioned it, I'm starved," he said.

Nikki looked thoughtful. "Well, I don't have anything to eat in the house, but some very nice neighbors live a few miles from here. I met them yesterday when I borrowed their telephone. Maybe they would loan me a some eggs or something." She reached for her tea and took a sip. "Why don't you take a shower and then lie back down for awhile. And after I fix you something to eat, I'll bring it up to you."

"Are you always this kind to strangers?"

Nikki chuckled "Only the ones I find on my property in need of help in the dead of night," she said.

"Lucky for me you spotted me, or I might not have made it through the night."

"You did lose a lot of blood. You may not be out of the woods yet," Nikki said.

Corbin's gaze studied Nikki's expression. "Maybe while you're at this neighbor of yours, you should send for a doctor."

"I don't personally know any doctors in the city, and the closest hospital is about an hour's drive. But maybe I could ask my neighbors if they know anyone…"

Corbin leaned across the table and patted Nikki's hand. "That's okay. Don't worry about it."

"Do you like eggs?" she asked, trying to lead her thoughts in a different direction.

Corbin smiled and said, "I don't remember, but at this point I think I could eat a horse, I'm so hungry."

She cringed at the thought. "I'm a vegetarian myself."

"What does that mean exactly?" He teased. "That you don't eat horse meat?"

"Yes," she replied. "Especially horse meat. Red meat will kill you," she added, with a nervous chuckle, suddenly aware she had used the word kill. Nikki stood up. "What shall I call you?" she asked, putting the empty teacups on the tray.

"Gee, I don't know," he said. "Why don't you choose a name for me? And while you're at it, why don't you tell me yours." He smiled, feeling strangely attracted to her.

Nikki said thoughtfully. "Let me see your hands." She leaned over and lifted Corbin's hands, and turned his palms downward. She studied them. "Now, shake my hand. You know, like we had just finalized a business transaction. Yes, that's it. A business handshake. Nice and firm. Good," she added, letting her gaze travel the length of Corbin's manly frame.

Corbin chuckled. "All that just to choose a name for me?" he asked, swallowing hard when their eyes met.

Nikki nodded. "A person's name can tell a lot about them."

"Really?" Corbin cocked his eyebrow.

"That's right. My father once told me that you could tell a man by his handshake and the kind of shoes he wears. I find that to be true of someone's name as well."

Corbin grinned. "Yeah? And what exactly does that mean?"

Nikki placed her hands on her hips. "Well, you have a nice firm handshake, which suggests to me that you're comfortable shaking hands. So, apparently, you shake a lot of hands. Perhaps you're a businessman of some type. Your fingernails have been manicured and lightly coated with a clear nail polish suggesting two things to me. You care about your appearance so you're accustomed to being around a lot of people. Image is very important to you. Secondly, you have money. Only the wealthiest of men are vain enough to have their nails polished."

"You can tell all that just by looking at my hands?" He shook his throbbing head. "Well, considering for a moment that you're right, it's good to know, at least I have money, because as you can plainly see, right now, I don't seem to own a pair of my own boxer shorts, "

Nikki removed her hands from her hips. "I have your clothes soaking," she offered. "I'm trying to get the blood out of your shirt. Your suit, by the way, comes from an expensive clothing store in London. The House of Duvall. Peter Duvall. Does his name ring a bell for you?" she asked, studying Corbin's expression.

"No, I'm afraid not." He shrugged. "But please don't name me Pierre. It just doesn't feel right." He cringed at the thought.

Nikki giggled. "No, actually I was thinking of a more manly type name. Maybe something like Frankie or Bruce. What do you think?"

"Those names sound more like hood names. You know, like bullies, bad guys, gangsters, and thugs." He paused, seeing the frightened look in Nikki's eyes. "What? You think I'm a hood?"

"No, of course not," she lied. "Even if you were a gangster or hit man, or something like that, what business is it of mine?"

"What? Now you think I go around killing people for money?"

"I didn't mean that exactly," she said, in an attempt to calm the handsome stranger.

A hurt look masked Corbin's face. "Well, then what exactly did you mean?"

"My name is Nikki. Nikki Rourke. And I am sorry if I upset you. I didn't mean too," she said. "Listen, how about we finish this conversation when you're feeling better? I think I should go in search of some food to feed you before you faint from starvation."

Corbin nodded. "I think that's a good idea. And while you're at it, try and find me a more suitable name, if you don't mind. I don't know who I am, but I doubt I go around whacking people," he said, attempting to rise to his feet.

Nikki glanced at him. "Are you going to lie down?"

Corbin turned to leave. "I think I should," he said. He glanced back over his shoulder. "Nikki, thanks for looking after me. And please don't be afraid of me. I won't hurt you."

CHAPTER **25**

Homicide Detective Charlie Miller chomped down hard on his day-old burnt piece of 'no cream if you please' toasted, whole wheat, breakfast bagel as he crumbled up and tossed its bag into the waste basket. He removed the lid to his extra strong espresso and felt around inside the outer pocket of his suit jacket for sugar substitute. After he stirred it into his coffee, he reached for the telephone and dialed the business number of Corbin Douglas.

Disappointed to learn the private investigator had not yet shown up for work, Charlie found his tiny phone book in a hidden compartment of his alligator skin wallet and opened it to his friend's unpublished number. He was disappointed again when Corbin didn't answer.

Charlie took another bite of his bagel before assigning several police detectives to track the private investigator down. It didn't take long to learn where Corbin's car had been parked all night.

"Okay, thanks Gillespie," Charlie said, putting the phone on its cradle. He grabbed his cup of Espresso and darted out of his office.

Once he was seated in the police car, he said. "Let's go, Cromwell."

Later, after checking the car out carefully Charlie said, "There doesn't seem to be any foul play here, but I still need to track Douglas down. I'm going to talk to his girlfriend, and the rest of you guys spread out and find him. Phone me the minute you do. It's important." Miller slammed the car door of the private detective's vintage Stingray.

*****

Regina Prescott yawned, stretched, and rolled onto her side to cuddle with her boyfriend, Corbin Douglas, but then she realized she wasn't home.

"Oh, shit! What have I done?" she complained, forcing herself to sit up. She glanced around her unfamiliar surroundings and released an angry sigh. "Damn it!" she groaned, removing the sheet from her naked body and getting out of her former lover's bed.

'If Corbin knew what Kramer and I did last night he'd kill the both of us.' Regina thought as she crossed the room to retrieve her clothing. 'What was I thinking?' She rushed to the bathroom to shower and dress.

In less than twenty minutes, Regina Prescott was ready to leave Kramer Davenport's luxurious, penthouse apartment, but she decided to phone her office first to see if Corbin Douglas had been trying to reach her. She picked up the telephone and sat down on the bed. She started to dial her office number, but hesitated when she heard Kramer raise his voice on the extension in the outer room. Instead of putting the receiver down, she listened in.

"Yeah. So what, Paul?" He growled at the caller on the other end of the phone line.

"Plenty if Mr. Juliano doesn't find that goddamn broad!"

Regina quickly recognized criminal attorney Paul Cucchiara's voice as he shouted into the receiver.

Kramer released a heavy sign. "I don't understand, Paul."

"The F.B.I. apparently has Mr. Juliano under a spy glass. I found out last night. Can't get into details right now, but we need to tie up some loose ends, and we need to do it quick!"

"Okay, but not over the phone like this. I'm not alone. I'll be in the office in about an hour. We'll talk then."

Regina put the receiver down after Paul Cucchiara clicked off. She turned to face her ex-lover as he entered the bedroom.

"Good morning, beautiful." Kramer greeted, as he crossed to room toward her.

Regina stood up, forced a smile, and turned her face slightly so he kissed her cheek instead of her lips. "Good morning, Kramer," she said, freeing herself from his embrace. "Why didn't you wake me before now? I have to go, "she said, lowering her eyes.

"Hey, slow down babe! What's wrong? You get up on the wrong side of the bed this morning, or what?" He pulled her back into his arms and kissed her.

After a brief struggle to free herself, Regina shoved him away. "Please, Kramer. I…I don't have time for this. I'm running late. I really do have to go." She forced a small grin.

Kramer shook his head in hurt dismay. "I guess our making love last night didn't mean anything to you."

Regina backed away from his caresses. "Kramer, I don't have time for insecurities this morning. I'm sorry about last night. It should never have happened."

"You are something else, Regina! A real piece of work. Last night you fuck my goddamn brains out, begging me for it. And this morning you won't give me a kiss. " he shouted heatedly.

Regina cleared her throat. "I was drunk last night, Kramer. I was pissed at Corbin, and you took advantage of the situation."

Kramer glared at her. "Are you saying I forced sex on you? I raped you?"

Regina released a sigh of frustration. "I didn't say that."

"You said I took advantage of you last night."

"What I said was, you took advantage of the situation. There's a difference, Kramer."

"Yeah, there's a goddamn difference, all right. When I asked you out for dinner, you could have said no. Why didn't you if you felt that strongly about it?"

"So it's my fault we had sex because I accepted your dinner invitation?"

"You could have asked me to stop when we were making out in the back seat of my car."

"You're right, Kramer. Maybe it was I who seduced you," she snapped.

Kramer tried to pull Regina to him, but she shoved his hands away. "Hey, Regina. I'm not trying to place blame here. I wanted you. You wanted me. We made love. What's the problem?"

Regina shook her head. "The problem is Corbin. I should've..."

Kramer interrupted Regina. "Hey, if you want to blame somebody for what happened between us last night then blame that son-of-a-bitch. He's the one that's not getting the job done, babe."

Regina fought back tears. "You know what, Kramer?" she asked. "You are an ass hole."

Kramer shrugged. "I like fucking you. So sue me."

Regina shook her head. "I never realized what a slime you are."

Kramer chuckled.

"Fuck you, Kramer. I'm out of here!" She flashed him a look of hatred on her way out, mumbling under her breath as she hailed a taxi.

After giving the driver directions to her downtown office, Regina glanced at her wrinkled clothing, feeling grateful that she always kept a change in her office for an emergency such as this.

CHAPTER **26**

Homicide Detective Charlie Miller sat patiently in the outer lobby of criminal attorney Regina Prescott's office going over the notes he had jotted down the evening before while talking to the employees that worked at the popular Jazz Club, the Blue Gibson, as he waited for the female attorney to arrive.

'Kyle, what's your last name son?'

'Nelson.'

'And how long have you worked at the Blue Gibson?'

'About five years now.'

'And the blonde singer that was up on stage tonight, who was she?'

'I'd rather not say, sir.'

'I see. Well, Kyle, you can either tell me who she is right now, while I'm here or..." He paused. 'Or you can go downtown and stay there until you do. The choice is up to you, son. Take your time and think about it.'

'All right." Kyle sighed. "Her name is Nikki Rourke.'

'Where can I reach her?'

The young bartender shook his head with uncertainty. 'I don't know. Nikki was supposed to be staying at the St. Regis Hotel while she was here in New York, but...' Kyle had paused to light a cigarette.

'Go on, Kyle. What were you saying?'

'Oh, nothing sir.'

'Why were you at the St. Regis this afternoon?'

A surprised expression covered Kyle's face. 'I wanted to see Nikki. She's in trouble and I wanted to help her.'

'What kind of trouble, son?'

Kyle took a long drag from his cigarette before answering. 'Someone wants to see Nikki dead.'

"Now, how on earth would you know something like that?' he had asked with growing interest.

'I just do.'

Charlie shook his head. 'Wanna try again?'

Kyle looked thoughtful for a few moments before responding. Finally he conceded. "All right. This broad I date told me.'

'Told you what exactly?'

'Told me that Nikki was in trouble.'

'And?' Charlie had asked in an attempt to get Kyle to continue.

'And nothing. That's it.' The young bartender shrugged.

'Details Kyle. I need lots more details," Charlie said, leveling his eyes at the young bartender.

'Damn it!' Kyle spat and then ran his fingers through his long hair.

'Like I said before Kyle, we can either do this here or take it down to the station. It's your choice.'

Kyle nodded, understanding the detective's threat, and once again conceded. 'This broad I date was at her friend's house about a week ago and needed to use the phone. When she picked up the receiver she overheard a conversation.'

'I see. Did your friend tell you about the conversation?'

Kyle nodded. 'She overheard her friend's husband talking to a woman. This woman was threatening him. She told her friend's husband that if he didn't come and see her soon that he would live to regret it, starting with Nikki Rourke as she stepped off the plane from London.'

'Is that all she said?'

'Yes.'

'And what is this friend's name?'

'I can't tell you. She's soon to be married. I don't want to get her into trouble.'

Charlie shook his head. 'Sorry son, it doesn't work that way. I need a name.'

Kyle ran his fingers over his mouth before giving in. "All right. Her name is Sidney Cox.'

'And what is Ms. Cox friend's name?'

'Who?' Kyle glanced at the detective with uncertainty.

'You said Ms. Cox was at a friend's house when she overheard the phone conversation.'

'Oh, yeah. Mrs. Gray. Her name is Jill Jefferies Gray.' The name stuck in his throat.

'Forrest Gray's wife?'

'That's right. My father…'

Charlie cut in. 'Yeah, I know, Kyle. Your father works for them as the family chauffeur.'

Kyle looked surprised.

The Shadow of Her Smile

'I have a few more questions for you tonight Kyle, and then I want you to stop down at the police station tomorrow afternoon in case I have more questions I might have forgotten to ask you tonight. All right? I'm telling you right now, son, I won't be a happy camper if I have to come looking for you. Do you understand?'

Kyle nodded. 'Yeah, sure. I'll be there. I'm not looking for trouble.'

'All right, Kyle,' Charlie said and then paused to collect his thoughts. 'You said your friend Ms. Cox overheard the threatening conversation about a week ago, right?'

Kyle nodded his head.

'Okay, son. Have you heard anything about a young woman that was shot and killed inside the airport in London about a week ago?'

'Yeah, sure. It scared the hell out of me. At first I thought it was Nikki." His eyes widened as he spoke. 'That happened the night after Sidney told me about the phone conversation she overheard.'

'Did you talk with Ms. Rourke after the young woman was killed?'

Kyle shook his head. 'No. I tried to of course, but she didn't return any of my calls.'

'Why?' Charlie asked.

'I don't know. I never got a chance to discuss it with her.'

'Tonight at the club was the first time you'd seen Ms. Rourke since Sidney told you about the telephone conversation?'

'Yeah, that's right. But we never had a chance to talk.'

'How'd you know where Ms. Rourke would be staying?'

'Nikki likes that hotel. It's always been one of her favorites. I had Sidney phone the hotel to see if Nikki had booked a room. As it turned out she had.'

'How'd you know when she was planning on being here in New York?'

'I ran into a friend of Nikki's, and she told me that she asked Nikki to help her out for a few weeks.'

'The name of the club is The Scarlet Ribbon, right?'

'That's right, Detective."

'How do you know Ms. Collins?'

'Nikki and I met Jacqueline about three years ago. In a way she stole Nikki from me.' He added.

Charlie shot the young bartender a curious glance. 'I don't understand.'

'Nikki and I were in love. Hopelessly in love. And Jacqueline came between us. The bitch took Nikki to France and turned her into a big star.'

Charlie looked thoughtful. 'Listen son, maybe you shouldn't be telling me this.'

'Huh? You don't think I…'

Charlie interrupted. 'Let's hope it doesn't come to that, Kyle.'

'What do you mean Detective? I don't understand.'

101

'You were telling me about Ms. Collins taking your girlfriend away from you.'

The young bartender jumped to his feet. 'I wouldn't touch a hair on Nikki's head. I love her.'

Charlie motioned for him to sit back down on the barstool. 'You strike me as a lover and not a killer.'

'Yeah. A lover. That's me all right.'

'Okay. Let's see. Oh, yeah. Do you remember seeing anyone suspicious at the St. Regis this afternoon while you were there?'

Kyle shrugged. 'I don't know what you mean.'

'Another woman? Perhaps a woman that resembles Mrs. Gray?'

'Mrs. Gray? What?' Kyle looked confused. 'Oh, wait a minute. You saw a woman going up to Nikki's room on one of the hotel tapes or something like that, right?'

The detective nodded. 'Something like that.'

'You must be talking about Sidney. She and Mrs. Gray look a great deal a like. I sent Sidney to tell Nikki to stop by the Jazz Club as soon as possible. I wanted to tell her about the conversation Sidney overheard. But Sidney said by the time she got to Nikki's room there were cops swarming all over the place.'

'Why did Ms. Cox get on the elevator at the seventh floor?'

Kyle shrugged. "You'll have to ask her that question when you talk to her. You are going to talk to Sidney aren't you Detective?' Kyle cringed at the thought.

'I have to.'

The bartender sighed. 'Tell her I'm sorry, okay?'

'Sure kid.'

'Will you ask Sidney to call me?'

Charlie cocked a brow. 'Don't push the favors.'

Kyle shrugged.

'How long has your father worked for the Gray's?'

'About twelve years or so, I guess. Maybe a little longer. Ever since the Gray's got married.'

'Do the Gray's get along okay together?'

'Sure. They get along just fine. That is, except for his wife's excessive spending habit. She drives him crazy with that sometimes.'

'Do they argue over it?'

'Constantly.'

'Does the arguing ever turn violent?'

'She always wins. He gives in. They kiss and make up. No big deal.'

'Forrest Gray is not a violent person?'

'No, he isn't.'

'Mr. Gray never wants to punish Mrs. Gray for spending his money?'

'Oh, sure. That's why he has so many mistresses. That's his way of getting even with her. Every time Mrs. Gray spends too much at Sotheby's he adds a new babe to his harem of beautiful women.

'Does Mrs. Gray know about… ?'

Kyle cut in. 'His mistresses?'

'Yeah, Kyle. Mr. Gray's mistresses.'

Kyle shrugged. 'Probably. Mr. Gray's not that clever. And Mrs. Gray is not stupid. Far from it. And she's far from an angel herself if you know what I mean.'

'What? You mean Mrs. Gray cheats on her husband too?'

'Sure.'

'Does Mr. Gray know?'

Kyle shook his head. 'Absolutely not. It would kill him. No matter what you think, Detective Miller, Mr. Gray does love her. So much in fact that every one of his mistresses resembles her.'

'No shit,' Charlie said, not understanding the logic.

'Of course, they're all a lot younger than Mrs. Gray. Well, that is except for Jacqueline Collins. To tell you the truth I think Jacqueline may have been Mr. Gray's first mistress.'

'No kidding?'

'I think Mr. Gray still see Jacqueline from time-to-time, but nothing like before.'

'How far back do Mr. Gray and Ms. Collins go, Kyle?'

'I'm not sure.' He shrugged. 'I was only a kid back then, but maybe about ten years.'

'Really?'

'Yeah. I remember Mr. Gray used to fly to France several times a week for a long time. I used to ride with my father to the airport to drop him off.'

'Has Mr. Gray seen Ms. Collins lately that you know of?'

Kyle nodded. 'He had me drop him off early this afternoon at her new club. He said he wanted to wish her good luck on the grand opening of The Scarlet Ribbon.'

'I see.'

Kyle glanced at his watch. 'Are we about finished, Detective? I need to let the employees go home. They're tired. It's been a long night.'

Charlie nodded. "Sure. But don't forget I want to see you tomorrow afternoon in my office.'

Kyle slid off the barstool and stretched. 'Sure Detective Miller. I'll be there.'

'One more thing before I leave, Kyle. Does Ms. Rourke have any family or friends that live in New York?'

'Nikki's family's estate is here. Rourke Manor in Quoque. The estate has been up for sale for some time now. Nikki's grandmother passed away a few years ago.'

'What about Ms. Rourke's mother and father?' Charlie asked with interest.

Kyle glanced at his watch again. "Nikki's father died a long time ago and her mother lives in London. She abandoned Nikki when Nikki was thirteen. Nikki was raised by an aunt but spent a lot of time with her grandmother at the family mansion in Quoque. Nikki doesn't have any family here anymore. Just me.'

'You said you think Ms. Rourke stopped by the Jazz Club tonight for your help?'

'Yes, like I said she has no one else.'

'And she knows someone is trying to kill her?'

'Yeah. Nikki just doesn't know who.'

'Do you think there might be a chance Ms. Rourke is hiding at her grandmother's estate?'

Kyle shrugged. 'Maybe. But I doubt it. I don't imagine anything is working right now. You know, like electricity? The couple that had been living in the mansion moved away about a year ago so Nikki put it up for sale.'

'Okay Kyle that should do it. For tonight, anyway. It's getting late. I guess you can send everyone home now. And I'll see you tomorrow.'

Charlie closed his note pad when Regina Prescott's secretary told him Regina would see him now.

Chapter 27

"Come on in., Charlie," Regina Prescott said and motioned the homicide detective to a chair.

Charlie nodded a friendly greeting as he crossed the room. "Sorry to inconvenience you, Regina."

Regina smiled. "Not a problem, Charlie. It's always nice to see you. What can I do for you?"

Charlie noticed the female attorney's puffy eyes. "Are you all right? You look as though you've been crying." Charlie's tone was one of concern.

Regina cleared her throat in an attempt to hold back her tears. "It's nothing. I'm okay, really. What can I do for you?"

"I was wondering if you have heard from Corbin this morning."

Regina shook her head. "No. I haven't. I haven't seen or talked to him since yesterday afternoon. Why?"

Charlie gave a sigh. "I'm having trouble tracking him down. I've been trying since late last night. I haven't even been to bed yet."

"I'm sure he's fine. I think he's working on a new case. He canceled another date with me last night," she said with an attitude as she drummed her long fingernails on her desk.

"Where was Corbin calling from when you talked to him?"

"He stopped by here," she said.

"I suppose you heard about the two young dancers that were murdered here in New York yesterday."

"Both redheads. One of them was murdered at the airport and the other at the St. Regis. Is that what Corbin's working on?"

"Not directly."

"When was the last time you talked to Corbin?"

"Last night. He and I went to the grand opening of a new club together."

Regina shot the detective an angry look. "Great! That's just what I needed to hear this morning. He stood me up last night to go on a date with you."

"Very funny, Regina. But it's not like that. I mean we didn't go there for a guy's night out or anything. It was business. The young woman Corbin is trying to track down was supposed to be at the club last night for the grand opening. But she sent a sub in her place. And guess what? This woman winds up getting her brains blown out the moment she steps off her flight."

Regina cringed at the horrible image.

Charlie sighed. "It gets worse. Want to hear it?" Regina nodded. Charlie went on. "Another dancer from London signed in at the St. Regis using this young woman's name and 'pop' she gets it in the back of her pretty head too."

"Jesus, Charlie!" Regina said.

"Yeah, I know. But I'm not finished. There's more." Charlie said. "A week ago at the airport in London another young woman, also a dancer, gets shot and killed as she was about to board her flight to New York and guess what?"

Regina shrugged. "You want me to take a wild guess?" Charlie nodded. Regina went on. "That young woman was a fill-in for Corbin's missing young woman, too?" Regina said, suspecting as much.

"That's right, counselor. After leaving The Scarlet Ribbon, I talked Corbin into stopping off for a nightcap at this Jazz Club I like to go to every once in awhile. And while we were there we got a glimpse of Corbin's missing beauty. Apparently, she was at the club disguised as a blues singer. Well, as it turns out, she got spooked and jumped off the stage, disappearing into thin air right before our eyes. Corbin took off after her and I haven't seen nor heard from him since. I'm concerned." He paused and then went on. "We found his Stingray parked across the street from the ferry that goes to Long Island."

Regina bit her lower lip. "You think Corbin's okay, Charlie?"

"To tell you the truth Regina, I'm getting worried. It's starting to look as if there might have been a hit put out on Corbin's missing dancer."

Regina's mouth flew open in stunned disbelief.

"Regina, I know this is none of my business, but Corbin was upset that you didn't leave a number where you could be reached last night."

Regina stopped Charlie. "No offense Charlie, but you're right. It is none of your business."

"Forget I said anything. But, there is something I'd like to share with you, just for the hell of it, if you don't mind."

"Shoot," she said, gesturing with a wave of her hand.

"I've heard that you've been keeping company with some very naughty boys." Charlie paused to choose his words carefully and noticed Regina suddenly flush. "The Feds have their eyes on them and they are close to bringing these bad boys down. I'd hate to see you pulled into something that could ruin your career just by association. In plain English, Regina I'd stay away from that –ex of yours if I were you."

"Thanks for your concern, Charlie. You're a good friend, but as you can see I'm a big girl now," she returned.

"Yeah well, be careful. I'm worried about you, that's all. I could get into trouble for telling you this much, understand?"

Regina nodded. "I know. It's just between us."

"Call me if you hear from Corbin."

"Sure, you do the same."

CHAPTER 28

Nikki Rourke hummed a tune while she prepared breakfast for herself and her unexpected house guest. 'I must be crazy,' she thought and stopped humming. 'I should be running out of this house as fast as my legs can carry me and hop on the next slow boat to China.'

Corbin Douglas stood inside the kitchen doorway, watching Nikki prepare their food. She occasionally talked to herself. Corbin smiled, as he enjoyed the sight.

The dancer was so lost in thought that she hadn't noticed her wounded house guest watching her every move.

"Okay, Nikki, that should just about do it," she whispered, crossing the room to the China Cabinet. She stood on tiptoe in an attempt to reach the piled-high stack of plates.

Corbin chuckled at her clumsy attempt and decided to offer her a helping hand. "Here, let me do that," he said.

Nikki turned to face him. "Been standing there long?" she asked, blushing. She stepped back a few inches to allow Corbin enough space to reach the plates.

"Long enough," he replied, as he handed Nikki two plates.

"You found me amusing, did you?" she asked as she made her way back to the kitchen counter.

"Entertaining would be more like it," he said, standing behind her. "Can I help?"

Nikki glanced over her shoulder and bit her lower lip as her eyes met his.

The expression on her face made Corbin swallow. He tried to calm himself.

Nikki could feel Corbin's warm breath on the nape of her neck as he continued to stand there gazing into her eyes. She shivered involuntarily. She cleared her throat and lowered her gaze. "Ah, sure. Here." She handed him the plates. She added, "All I have is tea."

"That's fine," he said.

"Well, here you go. Hope you enjoy it."

"The eggs smell terrific."

Nikki smiled.

"Is it okay if I just dive right in?"

"Oh, please do," Nikki invited with a wave of her hand.

Corbin swallowed his mouthful of food and glanced across the table at Nikki. "So, you still haven't decided on a name for me yet?"

Nikki gave him a puzzled look.

"A name. Remember? You were going to choose a name for me." Corbin said.

Nikki smiled. "Well, to tell you the truth I haven't given it much thought...

"How about now?"

"Sure," she said.

Corbin smiled.

"Unfortunately there's something we need to talk about first," Nikki said as she pushed her empty plate away.

"If you have something you need to get off your chest, then, please, just say it."

'To hell with it,' she thought, deciding to lay the cards on the table and be done with it. Nikki spent the following hour telling the P.I. about the horrible week she had just endured. A week that seemed to only get worse. Surprisingly, the more she talked to Corbin the more relaxed she became.

Corbin remained silent as she told her story.

"There's one more thing," Nikki said, standing up. "I have something to show you."

When Nikki returned she was carrying a gun several inches in front of her in its shoulder holster. She carried the weapon as though it were a dead mouse she was carrying by the tail instead of a gun in the holster. She hesitated before entering the room, and as a second thought, just to be on the safe side she removed the bullets from the weapon and slid them into her pocket. She handed Corbin the revolver. "Here," she said, forcing the gun on him. "This belongs to you. I took it from you when I was undressing you last night."

A confused expression crept across Corbin's face. He put the revolver on the table. "I see," he managed after a few moments. "I understand why you are afraid now, but I have no intention of hurting you. I don't know who I am, but killing someone...hell, anyone, especially a woman, just doesn't feel right to me." His tone was soft and low.

Nikki sat down at the table.

Corbin was thoughtful. "Nikki, did I have a wallet?" he asked. "Or anything else that might identify me?"

Nikki shook her head. "No," she said. "But you had a yellow envelope tucked inside one of your jacket pockets."

"What was inside the envelope?"

"It was a photograph of someone. A brief bio of that person, and a cashier's check for services rendered in the staggering amount of one-hundred-thousand dollars." Nikki watched Corbin's expression change to surprise.

Corbin was silent for a few moments. "You think I'm a hit man for the mob?"

"What else can I think? Put yourself in my place."

"Was the photograph inside the yellow envelope a picture of you?"

"Yes." Nikki wiped a tear from her eye.

"I understand how you must feel. Especially since there was a check inside the envelope too. The check had to be made out to someone." Corbin leveled his gaze on her. "What was the name on the check?"

"Corbin Douglas."

Corbin smiled as he watched her roll the name off her tongue again. "Corbin Douglas," he said. "Does that name suit me, Nikki?"

Nikki returned his smile and nodded.

"Corbin Douglas it is," he said shrugging. "Was there anything else inside the envelope?"

"No, that was it."

Corbin sighed. "Why don't you look in the telephone book and see if there is an address or phone number for Corbin Douglas listed?".

"That's a good idea!" Nikki exclaimed. She felt hopeful for the first time since they met.

His name wasn't listed.

Nikki slumped back down in her chair, was quiet for a few moments, and then offered in his defense, "But my grandmother's telephone directory is a couple of years old."

"I've been studying this automatic weapon, and if I were a hit man I think I'd prefer a different type of gun. Maybe something, I could get rid of at a moment's notice. Perhaps something with a silencer. I imagine I would want to make as little noise as possible after I killed someone. This type of gun is used mostly by cops," he added.

"Really?"

"Nikki, I'm no killer," he said. "You're going to have to take my word for it. Now, if you will excuse me, I think I should go and lie down for a while. My head is really starting to hurt. Thanks for breakfast."

"Corbin," Nikki said.

He turned to face her again, and as he did he suddenly felt lightheaded and dizzy. He grabbed for the back of his chair but staggered backwards instead. Nikki jumped up and a split second later, reached out and protectively pulled him close. Her rapid response startled him and he instinctively threw his arms around her and held on tightly.

"Are you okay, Corbin?" she asked.

"I need to lie down. Will you help me upstairs?"

In silence, she helped Corbin Douglas, up the long spiral staircase, one-step at a time, to her father's bedroom.

CHAPTER 29

The loud beeping of an automobile horn jarred Nikki Rourke from a lazy, dreamy state of unconsciousness to being wide-wake. She jumped to her feet, almost tripping over the rocking chair where she had been dozing. Before leaving the room, she glanced at the private detective, who was still sleeping.

She ran down one flight of stairs on her way to the second floor terrace to see what all the noise was about. She poked her head out cautiously, before walking onto the terrace and just as cautiously leaned over the skirting of the brass railing to see what was going on.

Recognizing the neighbors who had helped her, Nikki smiled, waved a warm greeting, and held up her index finger, indicating she would be right down.

"Great car!" Nikki said, admiring the pampered, candy-apple-red Model 'T' convertible sitting in her driveway.

Nikki's neighbors, Ellen and Howard Hollingsworth smiled. "Yes, it is. Howard was anxious to show off his prized possession." Ellen went on. "I hope we're not intruding, but we put a few things together for you. Some food, and a few other items that might come in handy until you get a chance to go to the store." She paused and then said, "I hope it was okay."

"Thank you, Ellen. It was very kind of you and Howard. I appreciate this so much. You can't begin to imagine," she said wrapping her arms around her neighbor's neck and giving her a hug. "You too, Howard. Thank you."

"The box of food items are in the trunk. I'll bring them in for you." Howard said as he slid out of the car and headed for the rear.

"Thank you," Nikki returned, and her gaze followed Howard as he started toward the house. "I'll get the door for you," Nikki said, jumping in front of her neighbor and shoving the door open.

Howard set the heavy box of groceries down on the kitchen counter as he glanced around the room. "I've always liked old Victorian houses like this one.

Too bad it wasn't up for sale before Ellen and I bought our house."

"I've always loved it too. I spent a lot of time here with my grandmother when I was a little girl." Nikki sighed at the memory.

Howard started walking in the direction of the dining room as he spoke. "It needs a bit of work, though."

"I'll have to take care of that the first chance I get." They continued to talk as Nikki led the way to the living room.

"You really should get the lock replaced on the entrance gate right away. You never know what might be wandering around outside at night." Howard wagged a finger at her in a fatherly manner. "There's already been two young women murdered in New York."

"I heard about it while I was out last night."

"Pity, two beautiful young girls like that." Howard shook his head sadly.

"Yes, it is Howard." Nikki said as she attempted to coax her friendly neighbor through the living room and out the front door.

She didn't see Corbin watching them from the bottom step of the staircase.

Howard paused on the front porch and looked back. "If it's okay with you Nikki, I'll send my handyman over to replace that lock on the front gate."

Nikki thanked him again before closing the front door.

"Help!" Corbin called out. "Please help me to the sofa. I feel woozy." He gestured in the direction of the sofa.

Nikki put one arm around his waist and the other across his shoulder as he leaned on her. Their gaze met and Nikki felt her heart suddenly begin to race. She shifted her gaze.

Once comfortably seated, Corbin cleared his throat. "Do you have anymore of that tea?" How he loved her smile. He wondered whether she knew how captivating it was.

Nikki nodded. "I also have wine. My grandmother had an extensive wine collection." She pointed in the direction of the antique wine cabinet.

"Wine would be perfect. Thank you."

"Are you a red Bordeaux or white Bordeaux kind of guy?" she asked.

Corbin chuckled. "Umm, I don't rightly know, ma'am, but oddly I feel as though I may be the type of man who likes it all."

Nikki smiled. "In that case might I suggest…" She paused as she traveled her long coral-colored fingernails across the top row of wine bottles as though she were giving each bottle thoughtful consideration.

He smiled, watching her make her selection with the greatest of care. Finally, she pulled a bottle from its resting place and smiled when her gaze found his. She cleared her throat and spoke as though there hadn't been a long pause.

"A 1988 red Bordeaux. Undoubtedly an excellent vintage." She smiled. "Particularly from those estates where the growers sat out late September storms and harvested the grapes in an exceptionally warm and sunny October." She paused, and licked her lips as though her taste buds had already sampled the harvested bottle of golden grapes that she was holding with great care.

"A mild, wet winter and spring necessitated widespread spraying and resulted in an uneven flowering. This was followed by a hot, dry summer which lasted from July through September of that year." She smiled again. "What do you think? Would you care to try some?" She dangled the bottle of wine in front of her as she awaited Corbin's response.

Corbin chuckled. "I'm impressed. Talk about someone who knows the wine industry!" He shook his head. "How could you possibly know something like that?"

Nikki giggled at the P.I.'s excitement. "My grandmother," she replied. "When I was a little girl, she taught me many things. Especially things that were a passion to her." Nikki uncorked the wine bottle as she continued to speak.

"Things like vintage wine, expensive perfumes, and of course, art." She poured two glasses of wine. "Grammy Rourke knew the best and worst years for wine. From 1890 an average year for wine, to her two favorite years, 1961 and 1988. A firm well-structured vintage, she would say." Nikki smiled at the memory and crossed the room carrying the two glasses of wine.

Corbin smiled as Nikki handed him a glass of wine. "She sounds like a wonderful grandmother. You're very lucky to have known someone like her."

Nikki smiled.

"Mmm, very nice. Thank you. It's an excellent selection." Corbin took another sip.

"Thanks. I was torn between this bottle of wine and a bottle of the 1961 Bordeaux," Nikki said, gazing wantonly into the P.I.'s sexy, royal blue eyes.

Corbin swallowed hard to break the trance he seemed to be falling into. "What? No history lesson on the 1961 vintage?" he asked.

Nikki shrugged. "I didn't feel like getting into the comparison of the 1945 vintage verses the 1961 vintage."

As he gazed with deep rapture into her eyes, she squirmed.

Feeling the need to put a safer distance between them, Nikki jumped to her feet and pointed to the painting on the wall. "See the portrait over the fireplace?"

"Your grandmother?" Corbin asked, sipping his wine.

Nikki nodded. "May I introduce you to my beautiful grandmother, Asia Rourke."

Corbin stood up and raised his wine glass in midair as he toasted, "To you Ms. Rourke. How very nice to meet you."

"That was charming, Corbin. And tastefully done." Nikki turned to face the portrait and also lifted her wine glass. "Yes, Grammy. To you."

They both took a sip of their wine.

"Nikki," Corbin said as he sat back down. "I'm sorry someone is trying to hurt you. I can't imagine why anyone would…"

She stopped him. "So far, I've managed to elude my enemies. Hopefully they won't come back."

Corbin leaned in her direction and patted her shoulder. "I may not be much in the way of protection for you, but I want you to know that whoever is trying to kill you will have to kill me first. I promise you that much." He handed her his empty wine glass for a refill, and asked, "Shall we have another?"

Chapter 30

Homicide Detective Charlie Miller examined the granite-like face of the man sitting across the desk from him.

"I hope you realize it's going to take a little more effort on your attorney's part and a whole shit load of Juliano's money to get you out on bail this time, Carmine." A smirk crossed Charlie's face. "We got you good. So good in fact that you'd be lucky if the judge takes mercy on your miserable ass and sentences you to die by lethal injection instead of letting you rot in jail for the next hundred or so years."

"Ah, fuck you. Miller! You ain't got shit." Carmine returned sarcastically.

A grin crossed Charlie's face as he continued to watch Asaro squirm.

"Like I said before Miller, Fuck you. I ain't sayin nothin!"

"That's okay. We don't need you to. We got you on tape, Carmine. As a matter of fact, the Feds have that slime bag boss of yours on tape too. They're on their way to pick him up now. You're both heading for the big-bake off down below, this time."

"What the fuck you talking about, Miller? You ain't got shit!" Carmine shot the homicide detective a look full of icy daggers.

"Sure we do, Carmine. Don't kid yourself. The Feds have so much on you and Juliano it would make your head spin. What? You don't believe me?" Charlie shrugged. "How about I introduce you to a couple of guys. Say hello to my little friends, amigo," Charlie said, nodding to the two men who had been standing outside his office door waiting for his introduction before entering the detective's office.

Carmine's mouth flew open in disbelief when he recognized the two undercover agents he knew as Eddie 'Styles' Costa and Joey Mezzogiorno. Two men he had thought worked for the Juliano crime family.

"No fuckin way, Miller," Carmine finally managed after a few uncomfortable moments.

"I want you to meet F.B.I. agents… On second thought," Charlie stopped before telling the mobster the real names of the two undercover agents. "Well, never mind their real names. You'll find that out soon enough Carmine." Charlie dismissed the two agents with a nod. "You guys can leave now. We'll turn him over to you shortly."

Carmine had paled.

"Got anything to say now, amigo?" Charlie asked.

"Why am I here, Miller?" Carmine's tone was nervous.

"I need answers. And I need them now!" Charlie barked, leveling his tired, angry eyes on the gangster.

Carmine responded with a wicked chuckle. "Answers, Miller? Get real. Why should I make your goddamn job any easier?"

Charlie gave a frustrated sigh. "Because, if you don't give me the answers I need, I'm personally going to tell Juliano you're the reason the Feds were able to nail his ass this time," Charlie countered.

Carmine laughed. "Yeah, right. Like Anthony is going to believe anything you guys have to say," he said with a smug grin.

Charlie shrugged. "You are the one who brought Joey and Eddie into the family."

"So what?"

"So, you fucked up. We'll convince Juliano that you sold out. Made a deal. Worked with the Feds. Plain and simple. Take my word for it, Carmine, Juliano will believe you went along with the program to save your own ass."

Carmine considered the detective's ultimatum. "What do you want answers to, Miller?"

"We know you were ordered to silence a young woman as she was getting off her flight in from London yesterday morning. Nikki Rourke. But instead of killing Ms. Rourke, some other young woman got it. We also know you didn't do it. Someone beat you to it, thinking the young woman who departed the plane was Ms. Rourke. We suspect the shooter was a woman. Who was she?"

"How the fuck should I know?"

"You at least have to have an opinion, Carmine."

"I don't know." Carmine shrugged.

"All right. Then tell me who put a buzz in Juliano's ear, telling him where Ms. Rourke would be staying while she was here in New York?"

"Some broad."

"Who?"

"Some broad he fucks once in awhile."

"Jacqueline Collins?"

"Naw. The other broad."

"Who?"

"Some rich broad."

"Sidney Cox?"

"No."

"Cut to the chase, Carmine. I need a name."

Carmine sighed and glared at the detective. "Gray. Jill Jefferies Gray," he said.

"Forrest Gray's wife?"

Carmine nodded. "Yeah. The billionaire's old lady. The bitch broke Anthony's heart when she married that rich son-of-a-bitch." Carmine's response was angry.

"Mrs. Gray used to be Juliano's woman?"

Carmine nodded. "That's right Miller."

Charlie chuckled. "No shit? That's amazing." He shook his head, smiled again, and continued. "I can't believe Juliano didn't have Mr. Gray popped for stealing his woman."

"Naw. Anthony loved her too much. He wanted the bitch to be happy."

"For a man like your boss, that must have been some kind of love he felt for her to let her get by with that." Charlie pulled out his pack of cigarettes, lit one, and offered one to the gangster.

Carmine accepted the cigarette. "Yeah, Anthony was nuts about her, all right. Still is. He can't stand to see her hurt."

"So you're saying what? That Mrs. Gray told Juliano about her husband's indiscretions and…"

"Something like that. I guess."

"Did Mrs. Gray make it a point to let Juliano know every time her husband broke her heart?"

"Pretty much. I told you, he still loves the broad. He'd do anything for her."

"Murder?" Charlie leveled his gaze on Carmine.

"Hey," Carmine shrugged.

"What about the young woman in London?"

"The Villano broad, you mean?"

"That's right, Carmine," Charlie nodded.

"What about her?"

"Did Juliano order a hit on her too?"

Carmine nodded slowly. "She wanted Mrs. Gray to give her a lot of money, or she was going to expose her secret past with Anthony. He couldn't let that happen."

"Un-huh. So who killed Rachel Ward and Gabrielle Graves?"

Carmine shrugged. "I told you. I don't know."

Charlie stubbed out his cigarette in the ashtray and then shoved it across his desk to Carmine. "Mrs. Gray?"

"I don't know. And anyway, why would she, when all she had to do was have

Anthony do it for her?"

"I see your point." Charlie paused briefly to digest everything Carmine had told him and then went on. "Tell me something, Carmine. Do you think Jacqueline Collins is capable of murder?"

Carmine laughed and gave a loud snort. "That fancy broad is capable of anything. Believe me, that woman knows how to get what she wants."

"Meaning?"

Carmine rubbed his hand around his mouth and carefully selected his words. "She's kind of like Mrs. Gray, in a way. She's got Anthony for a friend."

"If Ms. Collins wanted someone taken out of the picture permanently, she wouldn't have to do it herself?"

"Yeah, that's right, Miller."

"Why did Juliano want Nikki popped?"

"Because someone told him that the Villano broad told her about Mrs. Gray's past with him," he said, as if reasoning with a child.

"Okay, so if you didn't do it, and Mrs. Gray didn't do it, and Ms. Collins didn't do it, then just who in the hell killed Rachel Ward and Gabrielle Graves?" Charlie's fist punctuated his words as he hit the desk while he spoke.

Carmine shrugged. "I don't know, but I didn't say one of them broads didn't do it, Miller. I just said, why would they? Capesice?"

"Swell," Charlie mumbled, glancing at his watch.

"Are you done with me?" Carmine squirmed in his chair.

"Why?" Charlie asked with a sly grin. "It ain't like you got somewhere else to go anymore."

*****

Unable to get any more information out of Carmine Asaro, Detective Charlie Miller turned him over to the F.B.I. agents, glanced at the time with a tired sigh, popped his head out of the office, and called, "Has that young bartender from the Blue Gibson made it here yet?"

After learning Kyle Nelson had not stopped by the station, Charlie sent several police officers to bring him in. "And while you're at it, send a few more detectives out to bring in Forrest Gray and his wife, her best friend, Sidney Cox, and Jacqueline Collins. Tell them they might want to phone their attorneys. Oh, Hazel get in touch with someone from City Records, I want an address on a place called 'Rourke Manor' in Long Island. And Hazel," Charlie barked. "I want it like ten minutes ago!" Then he slammed the door to his office.

CHAPTER *31*

Homicide Detective Charlie Miller watched from the open door of his office as one by one Kyle Nelson, Sidney Cox, Jacqueline Collins, Jill Jefferies Gray, and Forrest Gray were escorted past him to a waiting room down the hall.

Unfortunately, he had already been informed by the small army of high-powered, high-dollar attorneys Forrest Gray had hired for all of them, that none of them had anything to say, since none of them knew anything about the murders of the two young dancers. Charlie was also told he was out of line in assuming that their clients knew anything about the murders, especially since the police department, or any other investigating facility had found no evidence whatsoever, linking any of the five people to the young women's deaths in any way, shape, or form. Charlie Miller didn't voice his final thought.

The frustrated detective watched his five suspects leave the police station one by one just as quickly as they had arrived. "Wonderful!" Charlie mumbled as he nodded to one of the young undercover detective's standing just outside his office. The young detective was part of a surveillance team the detective had put together to follow his five suspects after they left the police station. In Detective Charlie Miller's opinion, these people had motive, means, and opportunity to commit murder.

*****

Regina Prescott stood at the window of her seventh floor office and stared down the busy sidewalk filled with pedestrians. There had just been a three-car accident directly in front of her office building. Even on the seventh floor, Regina could hear the car horns beeping, radios blasting, and cursing from the street below.

She turned from the unsettling sight she had been staring at for the past fifteen minutes, crossed the room, circled her desk, and slammed her body down hard in her over-stuffed chair. "Damn it!" she groaned, still angry with herself for not being able to ease Corbin Douglas from her mind. Regina glanced at her watch and reached for the phone at the same time.

Moments later, she slammed the telephone back down for the fifth time that day, still unable to reach her lover. "Where the hell is he?" she asked, growing more and more worried with each passing hour. It wasn't like the P.I. not to at least phone his office during the day, even if he might have decided not to come in for whatever reason. She reached for the 5X7 photograph sitting on her desk and stared at his handsome face. She shook her head as her mind drifted back to a telephone conversation they'd had the morning before.

"Regina, I'm sorry. I'll run to the airport and when my surveillance subject gets off the plane I'll follow her to her hotel. Find out what room she'll be assigned to, and then I'll have Sam take over for a while. A plan well thought out and cleverly executed." Corbin had laughed and then went on. "At seven, I'll drop whatever I'm doing, run home, change, and pick you up. I promise."

"I know how you are, Corbin. You'll get involved and the next thing I know you'll be canceling another date with me," she had responded, while tapping her fingernails on her desk with growing irritation.

"I swear Regina, I'll be there. Trust me."

"I'm getting tired of you standing me up."

"You're making me feel bad. You know how it is in my line of work. At least you should know by now."

"I'm tired of being alone all the goddamn time!"

He did not respond.

"Corbin, you go and play your little spy games, but I'm telling you, if you stand me up tonight…"

He had interrupted, hating her threatening tone. "I'll have to phone you later."

"That damn man," she groaned, and set his photograph back down on her desk, as her thoughts shifted back to last evening when she was with her former lover, Kramer Davenport.

"I'm thrilled you changed your mind and decided to have dinner with me," Kramer had said, as he stood up when she approached the dinner table in the restaurant where she had agreed to meet him. Kramer walked around the table and pulled out her chair. After she was seated, he bent down and kissed her on the cheek.

"I didn't feel like eating alone tonight. And of course, I wanted to thank you for the lovely flowers you sent me today. And the day before that. And the day before that," she had said with a chuckle as she made a funny face.

He had laughed. "I had to see you. I made a mistake and I'm trying to make up for it with you."

She had chuckled. "You call fucking my best friend in our bed a mistake? I call it unforgivable."

"I fucked up, plain and simple, okay? Now, can we get past this? I miss you, damn it!"

She shook her head. "I've gone back to Corbin."

Regina remembered how angry her former lover became. She swallowed at the memory and continued thinking about the evening.

"What? You're fucking that goddamn nosy..." Kramer had begun to shout but she cut him off.

"Listen, Kramer. Who I fuck and don't fuck is my business. I didn't agree to have dinner with you tonight to discuss my sexual activities or lack of them, understand?"

Kramer cleared his throat. "Okay, I don't care why you decided to join me for dinner tonight, but I'm glad you did. Like I said Regina, I miss you." He then smiled that sexy come-hither smile that sent her heart racing.

Regina smiled at the memory. She remembered taking a deep breath as she tried to force the butterflies back down into the pit of her stomach. No matter the problems of their heated past, her former lover was fantastic in bed.

"Yes, a Manhattan would be nice, thank you." She had said, as her gaze traveled down Kramer's handsome face before stopping at his incredible full lips.

"Oh, shit! How could I have been so stupid?" Regina whispered and jarred herself back to reality.

She jumped to her feet as she reached for her purse, suddenly realizing she had forgotten to tell the homicide detective about the telephone conversation she had overheard between her former boyfriend and his law partner that morning. A split second later, Regina was on her way to the police station.

CHAPTER 32

Just when homicide Detective Charlie Miller thought his day couldn't get any worse, the district attorney, Bette Gerik, came charging into his office shouting. "News flash! Are you insane?" she spat, wagging her long, pointed, deep-plum colored fingernail in his face.

God, she was most attractive when she had her feathers all riled up like that, Charlie thought as he sat patiently waiting for her to stop flapping and come up for air.

He knew it was coming. Bottom line, he had jumped the gun. Screwed up big time, and he was getting his ass chewed out for having one of the wealthiest men in the world and his wife hauled in for questioning without permission from her highness the lovely D.A., the mayor, or anyone else with a rank higher than himself.

Bette continued. "Charlie, we can't make a case on speculation, circumstantial evidence, and gossip. What were you thinking? Hearsay just doesn't cut it!" she barked, calming down enough to take her wagging finger out of his face.

Charlie was surprised the D.A. had taken the time to come down and chew him out in person, instead of sending someone in her place, like she usually did, as of late, when they didn't see things eye-to-eye. For the past year, following their break-up, his former lover had made it a point to avoid him like the plague, and that had been just fine with him.

He couldn't bear to see her. The memories of their heated past would jump inside his head, and it would take days, weeks, even months sometimes for the sizzling memories to fade away.

"Are you listening to me, Charlie?" she snapped, seeing the distant look in his eyes as she continued to rake him over the hot coals. Charlie managed a nod as his gaze settled on her breasts. Bette noticed and her nipples hardened instinctively. She stopped talking when a quiet little voice inside her brain told her, move, run. Get out of the room while you still can. But her body was melting under Charlie's hot, sensual gaze. Bette silently prayed for a distraction. Anything to release her from the sensual hell he was unknowingly creating inside her with that hungry look in his eyes. A look that she remembered, too well.

The door to his office flew open, and a young police woman rushed into the room clutching a slip of paper.

Charlie said nothing, but continued to hold his former lover captive with his penetrating stare. Bette felt her face flush from the heat building inside her at an alarming speed. She couldn't seem to catch her breath. He noticed how flushed her face had become, and he smiled. Abruptly, he realized they couldn't just keep staring at one another. His heart couldn't take it. Charlie cleared his throat in an attempt to break this momentary spell.

The police officer realized she should have knocked first. She extended her hand and gave the detective the small piece of paper. "Sorry sir. But here's that address you've been waiting for all afternoon."

Charlie accepted the small piece of paper and smiled. His smile started Bette's heart rapidly pounding again. She forced herself to turn away.

"Thanks, Morgan," he said in a distracted tone.

Officer Morgan quickly left the room, closing the door behind her.

"I have to go." Charlie's voice was hoarse. He stood and grabbed his suit jacket from the back of his chair.

Bette cleared her throat. "Sure," she said leaning over to retrieve the handbag she had tossed onto a chair when she first entered the office.

Thinking the interruption had been for the best, Charlie started toward the door. "Later," he mumbled.

Bette stopped him from opening the door by grabbing his right arm. "Wait, Charlie," she said softly.

Charlie turned to face her, arching his eyebrows as he met her eyes. "What Bette? You want to chew my ass out some more?"

Bette stepped back from Charlie a few inches and closed her eyes in an attempt to choose her words carefully. "Charlie," she said. "I...I'm sorry. I didn't mean to yell at you like that. I was..."

Charlie stopped her. "Yes, but you did." He tried to shift his gaze away from Bette's full pouting lips. Unable to stop, he found himself wondering what it would be like to taste them again. God, how he missed kissing her, touching her, holding her.

Fiery sensations began to surge through Bette's body at his nearness. "No, really. I'm sorry."

"No, Bette. You're not sorry,' Charlie insisted, shaking his head. "You weren't yelling at me over this stupid case. Your shouting went far beyond that. It was personal. What do they call that?" Charlie paused as though he were searching for the proper words. "Misplaced anger. That's what they call it. This case didn't have a damn thing to do with it. You were yelling at me because you're still mad at me."

Bette's continued silence urged the detective on.

"And you know why you're still mad at me Bette?" he asked. He watched her fold her arms. "I'll tell you why, damn it!" he huffed, and released a frustrated sigh, as he leveled his hungry eyes on hers. "Because you miss me," he said, pulling her to him.

Bette shook her head. "No, it's not like that, Charlie," she murmured, but he silenced her with a kiss. She quickly pulled her head back and gazed into his eyes. "It's because I'm still in love with you…you big lug," she whispered tearfully and threw her arms around his neck.

"I've missed you something awful, Bette," Charlie said, holding her tightly. "What happened between us? I don't know anymore," he whispered. His warm breath caressed the side of her neck.

Bette freed herself from his embrace. "It was your inability to make a commitment Charlie, remember?" she said, stepping back a few inches. She folded her arms and gave him a hurt look.

Charlie turned and crossed the room to his desk. A mischievous grin covered his face as he opened a desk drawer. After several moments of fishing around inside the drawer, he pulled out a small, black velvet box and dangled it in front of himself.

"Commitment you say, Ms. District Attorney? You accuse me of jumping the gun. But it was you who tossed my belongings into the front yard before I got home with this little trinket."

"Oh, Charlie,' Bette squealed darting across the room. She threw herself into his arms. "Really? Is it what I think it is?"

Charlie smiled. "Well, I don't know. What do you think it is?" he asked, dangling the box above her head.

Bette snatched the box from Charlie's hand unable to wait a second longer. She opened it and cried. It was an engagement ring. "Charlie, it's beautiful," she whispered, showering his face with tiny kisses.

Charlie chuckled. "Does that mean you're not mad at me anymore?" he asked pulling her into his arms.

She glanced up at him with a bright smile. "I wouldn't say that exactly," she teased. "I mean, I haven't heard you mention a date yet, have I?"

"After I go and save Corbin Douglas's sorry rear, I'll have an hour or two free. How about then?"

Charlie's question became clear to Bette, she pushed him back. "What?" she squealed. "No wedding gown? My mother would kill me." She smiled. "How about we compromise? Why don't we make it the day after tomorrow, and I'll invite my mother to help me pick out a new white suit?"

Charlie smiled, nodded his agreement, and silenced her with another kiss.

CHAPTER 33

Outside on the terrace at Rourke Manor, Corbin leaned toward Nikki so that he could see her features more clearly in the darkness. Watching her, the P.I. was mesmerized by the young dancer's beguiling beauty. Her dove-white complexion, the provocative curve line leading to the nape of her neck. He moved his gaze upward. Her eyes so lovely in the moonlight and her smile. He ached to hold her in his arms. Could she be feeling the same way?

On impulse, Corbin pulled Nikki close, expecting her to pull away. Nikki's breathing quickened at his touch, but she didn't move.

He drew her even closer to himself, reveling in the chemistry between them. He could feel her tremble. Was it excitement or fear? He had to know.

For a moment, he hesitated, giving her a chance to back away, but instead, she moved closer to him and closed her eyes, anticipating his next move.

Gazing down at her closed eyes with long lashes curling against her creamy skin, he felt his heart begin to race madly. Corbin knew he was losing self-control.

An instant later, he pulled her to him and lowered his head. He pressed his lips to hers in a feather-like kiss. Corbin tasted the wine they had been drinking, still on her lips.

Nikki found herself wanting to back away, but she couldn't. His kiss had been seductive, suggestive, and she wanted more. She tossed away any thought of hesitation and pressed her mouth to his with eager urgency.

Corbin responded with an urgent need of his own. His chest felt hard and warm against her heaving, breasts.

When his mouth left hers, she moaned an objection, causing him to smile.

"Why did you stop?" she whispered along the side of his throat.

It sent shivers down his spine. "Nikki," Corbin groaned, and silenced her with another knee-buckling kiss. He continued to kiss her as he led her back into the house. Ever so slowly, as they moved, he could feel sexual tension building rapidly between them.

Inside the house, Corbin gazed into her eyes with desire. "Nikki," he whispered. "If we don't stop now, I won't be able too."

She smiled her incredibly captivating smile.

Trying to control himself, he waited what seemed like an eternity to hear her response.

"Do you want to stop, Corbin?" she asked.

He pulled her back into his arms, and kissed her deeply, passionately.

Suddenly, a loud banging on the front door jolted them apart.

"Corbin, are you in there?" Homicide Detective Charlie Miller shouted loudly into a microphone.

Corbin glanced at the beautiful young woman standing beside him. He was about to speak when the homicide detective shouted into the mike again. At that moment, a small army of police officers burst into the house and rushed up the staircase.

Corbin and Nikki stood staring at the activity around them until the homicide detective came rushing over to Corbin.

"Thank god you're all right," Charlie said, embracing the P.I. in a tight bear hug.

The stunned P.I. pushed him away.

Charlie stepped back a few inches. A hurt expression crossed his face. "What? Oh, the hug, hey amigo? Sorry about that, Corbin," he said. "It's just that I've been worried sick about you, goddamn it." He shook his head. "Why the hell didn't you call me?"

Corbin remained silent.

Charley sighed. "Hell, man. We've all been worried sick about your ugly ass. Especially Regina. So much in fact that she's down at the station right now waiting for me to bring you back."

Nikki and Corbin exchanged a glance. Charlie noticed. "Well? Say something." Charlie barked, feeling a little unappreciated.

Corbin gave the homicide detective a confused look. "Do I know you?' he finally managed.

At first, Charlie thought his friend was kidding. He laughed, shook his head, turned around in half-a circle, and then back again, before leveling his gaze on the P.I.

"Who are you?" Corbin asked.

"Oh shit! You're not teasing, are you? You really don't know who I am, do you?'

Corbin shook his head. "No," he returned as he continued to study the detective's expression.

Nikki walked over to Corbin and slid her arm around his waist. She looked at the homicide detective standing before them. "He's suffered a terrible blow to the head. And when he came to…"

Charlie interrupted. "Holy shit! Amnesia? You're telling me Corbin has amnesia?"

Nikki nodded. "That's right Detective. He doesn't remember a thing," she said.

Corbin smiled at her protective attitude and threw his arm around her shoulders.

"Why in Sam hell didn't you get him to a hospital?" Charlie snapped, noting there was obvious chemistry flowing between the couple.

Corbin shot Charlie an angry look. "Hey, you want to lighten up a little, Detective?"

Charlie shook his head and sighed. "Oh, shit! Come on, Corbin. I'm taking you to the hospital. I'll phone the station and have Regina meet us there."

"Who's Regina?" Corbin asked.

"His wife?" Nikki asked. She tried to remove her arm snuggly fitted around the P.I.'s waist, but Corbin stopped her. Their smiles connected.

Charlie noticed and frowned again. "No, Regina is not his wife. Not yet, anyway. She's his girlfriend," he explained.

"I'm going, too," Nikki retorted.

Corbin said, "Yes, Detective, Nikki is coming with me. As for that other woman you mentioned, you'll have to explain to her that I have no idea who she is."

"You can tell her yourself, amigo." Charlie shook his head remembering the temper of the P.I.'s girlfriend.

"I don't remember her," Corbin returned.

Charlie chuckled. "Don't worry about it amigo. Regina will have you remembering in no time, especially if you're with another woman." He shook his head, cringed, and mumbled the word "Ouch!"

Corbin glanced at Nikki. They shared another smile before he turned his attention back to the homicide detective. "It's Nikki that I want with me."

Charlie shook his head. "I need to bring Ms. Rourke in for questioning. Besides, she's still in danger," Charlie said with authority.

Victoria Taylor Murray

Chapter 34

Regina Prescott continued to pace back and forth inside Charlie Miller's office while waiting for him to return with her boyfriend. Not knowing whether her man at Rourke Manor was dead or alive was killing her. 'If he's not dead, then I'm going to kill him for scaring me half to death.' She thought as she continued to gaze around the detective's office. A photographed newspaper article cut, framed, and mounted on a wall caught her roving eye. It was an article about the homicide detective and her lover. The photo had been taken a few years earlier when they were still partners on the police force. She crossed the room to read the article.

Third year in a row homicide Detective Charlie Miller and Corbin Douglas share spot for "Detective of the Year award."

Regina spotted another mounted press clipping. 'Homicide Detectives Charlie Miller and Corbin Douglas receive special honors today at a ceremony held at city hall. The awards will be presented by Mayor Suzy Powell, Police Chief Morris Schiaffino, and Judge Tom Due. The awards are being presented to the detectives for their actions above and beyond the call of duty.'

The female attorney crossed her arms and moved on to the next press clipping. 'Today, our City holds its breath and joins in prayer for one of its own boys in blue. Awarded Detective of the year for the past five years, undercover agent Corbin Douglas was shot last night during a police sting operation in China Town. At this stage things are very serious according to Doctor Sanders at St. Elizabeth West Hospital, who was quoted as saying, "All any of us can do is pray. Things don't look good for Detective Douglas. We're not certain he will recover."'

"Oh, god," Regina cried at the painful memory. She turned her gaze to the office door when she heard someone enter. She quickly wiped a tear from her eye and cleared her throat.

Charlie entered the office without Corbin.

"Charlie?"

"He's fine. Well, maybe not fine, but…"

Regina's voice rang out in panic. "Spit it out before I have a heart attack!"

An instant later, Regina's gaze spotted the beautiful red haired dancer entering the office behind Charlie. The two women exchanged curious glances. Charlie noticed and ushered Nikki Rourke to a chair.

"Regina, this is Nikki Rourke. Ms. Rourke, this is Regina Prescott. Ms. Prescott is Mr. Douglas's girlfriend."

Regina nodded a greeting meant as the only civil thing to do. Without speaking to Nikki, she turned her attention back to the homicide detective. "So, where's Corbin, Charlie? What's going on?"

"I sent him to St. Elizabeth West Hospital to be checked out."

Regina's eyes widened and her mouth flew open. "What?" she asked. "Is he all right?"

Nikki squirmed in her seat as she continued to watch the homicide detective and the female attorney carry on their conversation while ignoring her presence.

Charlie shook his head and moved closer to the female attorney anticipating she would need a shoulder to cry on when he finished telling her about the P.I.'s memory loss.

It wasn't long before a tear escaped Regina's control and rolled down her cheek. "Amnesia? You mean to tell me that Corbin can't remember anything? Anything at all?"

"Except for me," Nikki reminded, sending a pointed dagger in the direction of the crazed woman who suddenly looked as if she were about to attack.

Charlie turned Regina to face him, and with his thumb wiped away a tear. "Why don't you let me have one of the police officers drive you to the hospital? Maybe seeing you will help."

Regina nodded her appreciation. "That's a good idea, but you and I still need to talk," she said.

*****

After Regina talked to Corbin's doctor, she began to feel more hopeful. She learned two things. Corbin was lucky to have survived the injury to his head. That was the good news. And the bad news was that Corbin had the young red-head to thank for it. It was the last part of the good doctor's statement that troubled Regina. The second and most encouraging thing Doctor Glavan told her about Corbin's condition was that after the swelling in his brain went down, the chances of his memory returning might look a little better. Bottom line, they couldn't be sure. With head injuries, especially serious ones like Corbin's, only time would tell.

Hiding a beautiful bouquet behind her back, Regina popped her head inside Corbin's hospital room. "Hi there," she said, cheerfully entering the room.

Corbin was sitting up in bed. He glanced in her direction. "Hello?"

Regina frowned. Without speaking, and crossed the room to put the flowers in an empty water pitcher. She set the pitcher down and turned to face her lover. "That looks nice. Don't you think?" She forced a smile.

"Yes, the flowers are nice."

Regina approached his bedside. She took his hand. She smiled and lowered her head to kiss him, but Corbin didn't respond. He pulled his hand free and turned his face. Regina fought back tears and sat down on the side of his bed. "You don't remember me do you, Corbin?" she asked in a hurt tone.

Corbin shook his head, turning his gaze toward her again. "I'm sorry, Miss. I have a memory that consists of the last ten hours or so," he said. He tried to force himself to study the features of the attractive woman sitting beside him.

"I see," she returned in a disappointed whisper and brushed at the strand of hair that fell in her face. "My name is Regina Prescott. Does that sound familiar to you?"

"No, it doesn't. But the police detective who brought me here mentioned earlier that someone was waiting for me at the police station. He said her name was Regina. Is that you?"

Regina smiled, but just as quickly frowned again, when a blank expression covered Corbin's face, and he once again pulled his hand away as she tried to hold it. "We're in love," she said softly.

"I'm sorry if you're hurt, but I have no idea who you are. I don't recognize you. You're a stranger to me. Where is Nikki?

Regina interrupted. "I won't allow you to see her again. I hold that young woman responsible for what happened to you."

Corbin shook his head. "You don't know anything about it," he objected. "She saved my life. Now, please leave. I want to rest." He turned his head away from her.

"Fine!' she snapped, jumping to her feet. She rushed to the door and glanced over her shoulder. "You can have her, but when you get your memory back, and I believe you will, don't come running back to me. You and I are finished!" She paused to clear her throat. Just as she did, Corbin's gaze turned to see if she had left the room, but she hadn't, and their eyes clashed. She gave an angry sigh. "This time Corbin, it's over between us for good!" Regina stuck her nose in the air and stormed out of his room.

"I can't believe that woman was my girlfriend!" He sighed. Perhaps it wouldn't be such a bad thing after all if he didn't get his memory back too soon. "I'm probably lucky to be rid of her and that god-awful temper," he whispered, as he glanced at the telephone. How could he get the homicide detective to bring Nikki Rourke back to him?

Chapter 35

The long intense argument was over, and the silence that replaced the loudness was madding. The only sounds that could now be heard throughout the mansion was the slamming of the front door as billionaire businessman Forrest Gray stormed out of the house, and the few final sniffles of tears Jill Jefferies Gray was trying to get under control as she stared into the antique mirror on her makeup table.

Jill blew her nose one final time, combed her beautiful, long, red hair, freshened her makeup, and changed clothes, before telephoning her friend.

A short time later, Jill asked Chapin to bring her silver-colored Mercedes Convertible to the front of the house. As the chauffer slid out of the car, Jill shoved past the employee, slid into the driver's seat, and peeled rubber for a quarter of a mile before letting up on the gas pedal. "Bastards!" she snapped, blaming her husband for starting the damn mess to begin with.

Jill suspected her husband had gone to the Scarlet Ribbon to soothe the ruffled feathers of his number one mistress. She knew her husband better than anyone, especially his five whores. She had known about them all along, starting with Jacqueline Collins. Jill may have been labeled many things in her life before marrying her billionaire husband, but stupid wasn't one of them. As long as her husband didn't make the mistake of getting one of his play toys pregnant, Jill was more than willing to turn a blind eye to his indiscretions.

Jill had only married him for his money anyway. She was far from an angel herself, even though, in her husband's eyes, she was certainly one, and to her that was all that mattered.

Marriage hadn't kept Jill from secretly living the exciting life she had so loved before her marriage to Forrest Gray. She just had to be discrete about it. And Jill was certainly that. There was no way in hell she was going to risk losing her husband's billions. Jill had schemed long and hard to get Forrest to propose, and she had no intention of giving him up. That, of course, meant one thing. Jill had to stay married to him. "Happy or not," was something she had not allowed herself to consider, especially since he made her sign a prenuptial agreement before the "I do's."

Sexually her billionaire husband was boring, a quick minute at best, but Jill knew she could get sex anywhere with anyone she chose. Her husband did, so why couldn't she? "What's good for the goose," was her motto.

Jill pulled her car up to the valet at Trump Towers and slid out of the seat as he opened the car door. She smiled and handed him a folded fifty-dollar bill. "I'll be about an hour," she said, and then turned away. She glanced back over her shoulder at the cute valet and smiled mischievously when their gaze met. "Make that an hour or two," she added with a wink.

The valet felt his face flush. He smiled, gave an understanding nod, and jumped inside the Mercedes.

Jill made her way to the lower level cocktail lounge where she spotted her friend, pacing back and forth. He smiled when he saw Jill approaching down the hall. "I was afraid you'd changed your mind," high-power attorney Paul Cucchiara, said, leaning in her direction to kiss her.

Jill extended her arm to stop him. "Please, not in the hallway, Paul. Did you get the room?"

Paul nodded. "If Anthony finds out about this he'll…"

"I don't think we have to worry about him anymore," she returned with a chuckle.

"I thought you knew Anthony better than that Jill. A jail cell doesn't stop a man like that from giving an order."

"Oh please, Paul. Anthony is not the man we used to know. He's become weak and careless. I'm not surprised he finally got nailed."

Paul nodded in agreement to her assessment of the mobster. "I agree. I just hope falling in love with you doesn't have the same effect on me, Jill," he whispered in a low voice and pulled her into his arms.

This time Jill didn't pull away. With her desire rising, she gazed into the criminal attorney's eyes. "What do you mean by that remark, Paul?" Her tone was soft and seductive.

"Falling in love with you has made Anthony weak. Staying in love with you all these years has made him careless. And his never-ending love for you has made him sloppy."

Jill chuckled. "And in my eyes, stupid." She pulled free from Paul's embrace. "Well, are we going to stand here in the hall talking all night, or are we going to the room to negotiate the favor I need you to do for me?"

*****

Nikki Rourke slipped out of the police station after homicide Detective Charlie

Miller excused himself and told her he would be back in a few moments. At the street, Nikki hailed a taxi. She instructed the driver to take her to St. Elizabeth Hospital West on York and Sixty-Eighth. A short time later, Nikki left the hospital, cursing under her breath, after being told the private investigator had secretly left the building.

Afraid to telephone Forrest Gray, Jacqueline Collins, or her former boyfriend, Kyle Nelson, the young dancer hailed another taxi. She wanted to go back to her grandmother's estate and get the tape recordings she had made before she went in search of a new place to hide.

Nikki was terrified, not knowing where to look for help. She began to cry. Her life had been turned upside down. She had no idea what she was going to do, where she was going to go, or who she could trust, that is, except for the stranger she had known for less than twenty-four hours, "Corbin Douglas." She felt her face flush at the thought of his name.

By the time the taxi arrived at the Long Island Ferry, Nikki was too late. It had just left. Now she would have to wait for the ferry to return. "Oh, damn!" she murmured. She glanced around her surroundings, spotted an all night diner, noted the time, and began walking.

*****

Corbin had no way of knowing he had just missed bumping into Nikki by a matter of only minutes. He glanced out over the rippling water and let his mind drift.

The whole time he was on the ferry he thought of nothing else but the beautiful young woman that continued to hold his heart captive with her charm, kindness, and her captivating smile. "That smile," he whispered in a torment of longing for her.

He understood he never really knew Nikki. She was a stranger to him. Corbin had been told that by the homicide detective claiming to be his friend. This man known as Charlie Miller had also filled him in on many things about his past, or a large part of it. He told him how they were once partners together on the police force, and Charlie was also kind enough to tell him a little about the present. Corbin was surprised to learn that his chosen field of employment was that of a P.I. and, according to the homicide detective, not just any private investigator, but a famous one at that. One of the best in the country. Charlie also filled him in on his relationship with "dragon lady," the hot-tempered female attorney he had met at the hospital, Regina something-or-another. "No way!" Corbin cringed at the thought.

So how come he didn't recognize this dragon lady if he was supposed to be that much in love with her? How come he didn't recognize the police detective if they were supposed to be best friends? How come he couldn't remember one damn thing his cop friend tried to share with him? "Very confusing," he murmured.

All the P.I. knew was that his memories were centered around Nikki Rourke. She had saved his life, and as far as he was concerned, he owed her. One way or another, he would find her and help her get out of the mess she was in. And after he did, just maybe, they could share a few more memories together.

"God, that smile!" he whispered again as the ferry docked, jarring his wandering mind back to the present.

Later that night, Corbin tried to focus on one goal. That goal was finding Nikki Rourke and keeping her safe and out of harms way. Before Corbin left the hospital, he had placed a telephone call to the New York Police Department and had a talk with his supposed friend and former partner in fighting crime, Detective Charlie Miller.

After a lengthy discussion and a thorough ass chewing for the way Corbin had so unfairly treated his supposed girlfriend, Regina Prescott, at the hospital earlier, Charlie Miller informed him that Nikki Rourke had managed to sneak out of the police station when he excused himself to go to the restroom.

Corbin smiled as he remembered his response to Charlie after chewing his rear out over the female attorney. "Sorry about Dragon Lady's luck. I'm sorry if I hurt her feelings, but I don't remember her, you, or anyone else right now. The only memory I do recall is that of a young woman who saved my life. She's also in a great deal of danger, and I mean to find her." Corbin dropped the receiver, jumped to his feet, and left his hospital room.

*****

Sidney Cox released a sigh as she entered her apartment. She closed the door and let her body fall against it as she began to sob.

The ringing of the telephone stopped Sidney's crying as swiftly as it had begun. She switched on the lamp and crossed the room to the well-stocked wet bar to answer the telephone.

The caller was the wedding coordinator from Gateau de Mers, Tinker French. Tinker told Sidney that she had not been able to think of anything except her since the night they spent together.

Stunned by Tinker's confession, Sidney laughed and rejected her. "Don't be ridiculous, Tinker. We shared nothing more than a quick minute, understand?"

After a few heated exchanges between the two women, out of hurt despair in her need to be with Sidney again, Tinker resorted to blackmail to get her way with Sidney. Sidney was stunned to learn that her nosy, new friend had taped their entire evening together.

"The pillow talk we shared will surprise you, Sidney. Every moan, groan, and yes, even your secret confessions were recorded." Tinker paused to clear her throat. "And if I were you, from this moment on, I'd go out of my way to try and keep me happy. Do you understand what I am trying to say?" Tinker threatened.

Curious as to what was actually on the tape recording, Sidney agreed to let the gay wedding coordinator come to her apartment and play the tape for her.

*****

Corbin had no problem letting himself into the estate grounds of Rourke Manor. Nikki's neighbors Howard and Ellen Hollingsworth had sent their handyman to replace the broken lock on the entrance gate and left the new key in the mailbox. After unlocking the gate, Corbin replaced the key, just in case Nikki decided to return to her grandmother's estate. It was something Corbin could only hope for at this point. Once inside the mansion, Corbin helped himself to another bottle of vintage wine from Asia Rourke's priceless collection. He smiled as he opened the 1988 red Bordeaux, recalling word for word, how Nikki had methodically described the treasured bottle of wine.

Corbin poured himself a glass of wine and walked over to the painting of Asia Rourke. "To you Ms. Rourke. You have excellent taste in wine," he said, toasting the portrait. "You also have a lovely granddaughter," he added. "One who is in terrible danger at the moment."

Corbin took another sip of his wine and went back to the bar to retrieve the bottle he intended to take upstairs with him. He wanted to snoop around a little inside the bedroom Nikki had been occupying, in an attempt to find something that might lead him to the beautiful damsel in distress.

After looking around her bedroom and not finding any clues as to where Nikki may have gone, Corbin decided to finish his fine bottle of wine out on the second floor terrace under the moonlit sky. As he walked out onto the terrace, he spotted a shoebox on the patio table. Corbin opened the box and removed its contents. In numbered order, Corbin stacked the fifteen tapes. He stared at them as he sat down and poured himself another glass of wine. After several swallows of the red Bordeaux, he shoved tape number one into the tape player.

By the time he had listened to all fifteen tape recordings Corbin could feel his boiling blood surge throughout his body. Nikki had been right all along. One of the people mentioned on the tapes wanted to see Nikki dead. Corbin was now sure of it. But which one?

Forrest Gray immediately got his vote. Why would anyone pay a hundred grand to find somebody, unless they were up to no good? And if Nikki and her billionaire sugar daddy were in love, then why hadn't she gotten in touch with him after she arrived in New York? It was as clear as the nose on the P.I.'s handsome face. Nikki didn't trust him. Many questions began to pop inside

Corbin's tired brain.

Corbin felt a sudden chill in the air. He drank the last drop of the wine before deciding to call it a night. He placed the tape recordings back inside the shoebox and took the box with him to the bedroom. He was tempted to sleep in Nikki's bed, longing to be with her, touch her, taste her, and make love to her. As a second thought, he decided against it. The scent of her expensive perfume on the pillowcase would be more than he could bear. Sleep was what he needed most. He had a case to solve, a young woman to find, and a murderer to uncover. And he couldn't do anything without some sleep.

CHAPTER 36

The night air stirring briskly throughout the bedroom, Corbin could smell the saltwater along the southern shoreline. He shifted restlessly in bed trying to get comfortable enough to sleep. But it was useless. As hard as he tried to shut his eyes, they would snap open again just moments later, and he stared at the cracked and stained ceiling as his mind kept playing over and over the fifteen tapes he had spent the past several hours listening to.

Between the disturbing tapes and his ever-building need to be with the beautiful, young dancer, whenever Corbin did manage to close his eyes for a few moments, he would be back on the terrace holding Nikki in his arms feeling overwhelmed by the touch of his hands on her flesh and the sweet, fruity taste of wine on her full, inviting lips. How he longed to kiss her again. His mouth enveloping hers. Their tongues searching, exploring, tasting one another.

He groaned at the heated memory and tossed his bed sheet aside. He was on fire. His body filled with frustrated desire. Unable to stand it any longer, Corbin got out of bed, wandered to the window, and pressed his forehead to the cool French plate glass. He stared into the darkness, wishing Nikki would come home. He could smell the on-coming rain in the air. He ran his fingers through his thick, dark-brown hair as he turned from the window, walked back to the bed, and threw himself down on it. He released a sigh of frustration and tried to force his eyes shut again. But it was to no avail.

*****

The rain was falling fast and furious. The cool damp breeze felt good, spraying raindrops off Jill Jefferies Gray's umbrella, falling against the warm flesh of her arms and face, as she made a run for it from her silver Mercedes to the front door of the family mansion.

The Gray's head butler jerked the doublewide doors open for the lady of the house to enter. "Allow me, Mrs. Gray," Scottsdale said, taking the wet umbrella from her trembling hands.

"Thanks, Scottsdale," she said, walking past. "Has Mr. Gray gone to bed yet?" she added, glancing back over her shoulder, as she continued walking toward the hallway leading to her husband's private study.

"Yes, Madam. Mr. Gray said to tell you that he would be sleeping in his private bedroom tonight and not to wake him. He has an early appointment tomorrow morning."

"I see." Her tone was curious. "Good night, Scottsdale," she said, rounding the corner of the hallway.

Jill walked into the study, mumbling under her breath, and closed the door. "Two down and two to go. Better make that three down and two to go," she whispered as her gaze caught the headlines on the front page of the evening newspaper lying on her husband's desk. She wished all of her husband's mistresses would suddenly drop dead.

She crossed the room and stood in front of the drawing mounted on the South wall of the study. A French drawing by Jean de Gourmont, entitled, "Massacre of Innocence." Her gaze studied the skillful style of the French artist.

Several moments later, she tugged on the right corner of the drawing, revealing a hidden wall safe she had secretly installed six months earlier, while her husband was away on one of his weekend jaunts to France, visiting his ever-growing harem of young, beautiful mistresses.

"Bastard!" She spat heatedly, as she opened the safe and removed a large, white file folder. Jill laid the file down on the desk, went to the wet bar, and helped herself to a double shot of Brandy. After several small sips of the strong tasting liquor, she returned to the desk and fell into its comfortable chair. She kicked off her high-heels and reached across the desk for her purse. She opened it, pulled out a pack of cigarettes, and lit one, before opening the folder. She began to read the contents. Moments later, she dropped the folder and the newspaper onto the floor and began to weep.

*****

"He's perfect," Nikki Rourke whispered, standing inside the doorway of Corbin Douglas bedroom. Her gaze traveled the length of his body. She relished the muscles in his strong shoulders and arms, his firm, flat stomach, thin waist and narrow hips. Her gaze lowered to view his strong thighs and legs then moved back upward. He stirred and stretched seductively showing off his muscular biceps in his sleep and causing Nikki's heart to beat rapidly.

She entered the room and paused at the bed, staring lustfully down at him.

She sucked in her breath when he opened his eyes and smiled. "Hi, there," she whispered.

Astonished, Corbin sat up in bed. "Hello yourself," he said, returning the lustful gaze with his own.

"I've' been looking everywhere for you, Detective," she said, sitting on the bed next to him.

Corbin continued to gaze at Nikki, unable to reply, and then he pulled her to him and kissed her.

Hot shivers ran down her spine. "Corbin," she panted, removing his hand, and suggestively placing it on her heaving breast.

"Does this mean..."

"Yes," she whispered.

An instant later, Corbin had Nikki undressed not knowing or caring how it happened. All that mattered was that they were together, and he wanted to make love to her. His body ached to join hers. He wanted to explore all of her. He needed to know if her need was as urgent as his. But he forced himself to slow down. His fingers clutched hers as he began to run fiery hot kisses down the nape of her neck to her shoulders and down to her perfect breasts, sucking one nipple at a time into his mouth, causing her to moan with eager anticipation.

He stopped kissing her and began to stare at the woman lying beneath him. She was beautiful. She was more than beautiful. She was magnificent. She was small boned and slender. Thick red hair curled to seductively fall below her shoulders. Perfectly shaped nose and full lips and seductive smile,

"Nikki, I love your smile," he whispered, and traced the outline of her mouth with his index finger, which made her shiver with heated desire.

Nikki silenced him with a kiss, as she changed places with him, shifting her lightweight body on top of his. "I must be dreaming," he teased, whispering in her ear with his warm breath.

Nikki was so beautiful that Corbin had to force the millions of butterflies back down into his stomach, as he continued to enjoy her gentle touches and wet erotic kisses. Nikki was young but an expert lover. No wonder Forrest Gray was more than happy to pay a hundred grand to find her and bring her back to him.

The animal-want in both of them was fiery, demanding, and explosive. Moments later, they shouted their uncontrollable releases together and then collapsed into one another's arms.

CHAPTER 37

Regina Prescott poured herself another shot of bourbon and staggered out onto the balcony of her penthouse condo. She downed the drink in one swallow. "Corbin, you son-of-a-bitch!" she hissed.

As she stared at the silhouetted city of lights below, her thoughts shifted to her conversation with her lover from several days earlier. Prior to their conversation, Regina was determined she was going to get the P.I. to propose to her. It was something she had wanted for a very long time. She wasn't getting any younger, she wanted to be married, settle down, and raise a couple of children.

"You know, Corbin, all my life I've been a no-nonsense kind of a person, goal oriented and practical. Even in college, I set goals for myself and knew what it was that I wanted to do with my life. Unlike most of my friends and classmates at Harvard, I wanted to make it on my own. Make a name for myself, one that I could be proud of. And I've done that the hard way. Unlike Rita, Royce, Laura, and Charlotte." Regina remembered she had released a sigh and walked to the window in her office and glanced out of it as she continued to speak.

"All four of my friends in college took the easy route and married into money and status. They settled. Not bad choices you understand. Rita's husband is running for Mayor this term an almost certain shoe-in. Royce's husband recently signed a contract for up and coming Mini Series with CBS. Laura is presently on super rich hubby number three and currently traveling around the world for the forth time in her life." Regina recalled. "And Charlotte's husband recently opened his tenth fast food chain in China."

Corbin scratched the side of his head. "Settled? You call that settling?"

"In my opinion. Yes."

Corbin shrugged. "I don't get it."

"You really don't get it, do you?"

Corbin stood and crossed the room. He wrapped his arms around her waist.

"I'm sorry, Regina. I don't understand what you're trying to tell me. Keep it simple, huh?"

She had freed herself from Corbin's embrace, stepped back a few steps, and folded her arms. "Corbin what I'm trying to say is that in my opinion my friends have been living their husband's lives and not their own."

"Your point?"

She shook her head and walked to her desk. "I've lived my own life. I've accomplished everything I set out to do," she said and pulled her chair out and sat down. "Except…"

Corbin glanced at the time. "Regina are you trying to make a point? Honey, I don't have time for guessing games today."

She had pushed his hand away and shook her head with irritation. "Corbin sometimes you can be an insensitive dick."

Then her secretary entered the office. "Excuse me, Ms. Prescott."

"Yes, Sela. What is it?"

"It's Mr. Davenport. He's in the lobby waiting to see you. He says it's important."

She had shared a glance with Corbin, and then Corbin shook his head and sighed.

"Thank you Sela. Tell Kramer I'll see him in a few minutes." She stood up, and told Corbin. "We'll have to finish this conversation later."

"You expect me to leave just because your 'ex' pops in for the hell of it?"

"You've been trying to get out of here from the moment you arrived." Corbin protested.

"You haven't taken your eyes off that damn watch since you walked in." He shrugged. "Fine, I'm out of here."

Regina reached out for Corbin's arm to stop him from leaving. He turned to face her. "Wait a minute. Why did you stop by my office this morning anyway? To break another dinner date?" She looked at him suspiciously

His face flushed. "I can't help it. I came to tell you that I've accepted a new case and…"

"Shit, I knew it!" she shouted, and slammed her body back down into her well-padded chair.

"Don't be like this. It's the damn business I'm in," he said, walking around her desk and sitting on top of it. He reached for her hand and she reluctantly gave it to him. He pulled her up and into his arms. "I'll call you later," he said, and kissed her.

The female attorney shook her head to bring her thoughts back to the present. She wiped a tear from her eye and released a deep sigh of regret. "Damn, you, Corbin," she spat again and drunkenly staggered back inside her apartment.

As Regina was rounding the wet bar to pour herself another shot of bourbon, the intercom buzzed loudly. She forced her tears to go away. After clearing her throat, she went to the security monitor and switched it on. "Shit!" she groaned, recognizing Kramer Davenport. She shook her head, causing her to almost lose her balance. "Damn it!" she cursed and pressed the button on the intercom. "What the hell do you want, Kramer?" she slurred.

The criminal attorney chuckled, realizing his former lover's condition. "Hi baby. I just wanted to stop by and apologize for my behavior this morning." His tone was soft and seductive.

"I-just want to be alone right now. I have some things to work out and I need to..."

"Please, baby, don't turn me away. I need to see you. Please Regina."

Regina knew she would probably wake up in the morning hating herself all over again, but she was drunk, she was hurt, and she was feeling vulnerable. But most of all she needed to be held. She sighed and loosened the belt from around her robe to reveal her nude body before releasing the lock, allowing Kramer Davenport clear access to her apartment. Her former lover may have been a lot of things the female attorney loathed in a man, but as a lover, he was incredible.

Regina turned from the door after opening it and slowly went back to the bar to pour herself and her guest a shot of strong liquor.

Chapter 38

Corbin and Nikki had fallen in love with one another and spent the past ten days making love. Corbin could have cared less if he ever got his memory back. No one from his past could have possibly meant as much to him as Nikki Rourke. The wonder of it all was that Nikki felt the same way about him.

*****

Homicide Detective Charlie Miller allowed himself as much time as he could manage with his beautiful new bride of a week. As far as solving the murders of Rachel Ward and Gabrielle Graves, the experts were still working on what little evidence they had collected at the scenes of both murders, as well as working on their own individual theories in trying to connect the five suspects. Without having any tangible evidence linking any of them to the actual murders, they seemed to be at a dead end.

*****

Forrest Gray and his wife, continuing their façade of a happy marriage, were busy putting together the final preparations for the wedding of Jill's best friend, which was to occur in two days. As for the future Mrs. Warner, Sidney Cox, she was busy at work attending to the last minute things that her wedding coordinator was supposed to be doing, but couldn't because of her sudden and mysterious disappearance.

*****

Corbin stood behind Nikki embracing her as they gazed out at the large pond from the second story terrace of her grandmother's old Victorian Mansion. Nikki loved the way his arms felt wrapped around her. It made her feel safe and warm inside.

Corbin lowered his head and kissed her hair. "Nikki," he whispered. "I wish we could stay here, wrapped inside one another's embrace forever."

She nodded and gave a content sigh. "Me too, Corbin."

Corbin swallowed. "There's something I-I want to say to you. I've actually been trying to get my nerve up all night," he confessed.

Nikki turned to face him. "You've got your memory back, haven't you?" she asked with a touch of sadness in her tone.

He lifted her hand to his mouth and kissed it. "Yes. Well, at least that's part of it."

"Oh?"

Corbin cleared his throat. "I want you to know, that I'm in love with you," he said. "Our past doesn't bother me," he confessed.

Nikki's mouth flew open in surprise. "Really?"

"Will you marry me?"

Nikki smiled her sexy smile. It always excited the P.I. "Yes. Corbin, I will," she squealed, jumping into his arms. They kissed, while the private detective carried her inside.

After several hours of making love, they took a long, hot shower together, and went to the kitchen to fix something to eat.

"You known, Nikki, I wasn't kidding about getting married. I want to do it right away. I don't want to risk you changing your mind," he said pulling her away from the stove.

"No chance of that. How about today?"

"Perfect. I have a judge friend that would be happy to do the honors," he said with a chuckle.

"But I've always had my heart set on a church wedding. Either that or getting married right here in my grandmother's home.

Corbin gave an understanding smile. "I see. We could get married here I suppose, but with all the repairs, your grandmother's house needs, well... I just wanted us to marry as quickly as possible."

"Today. We'll have your judge friend do the honors. And on our first wedding anniversary, we can marry all over again right here at Rourke Manor." Nikki said smiling. "Corbin. I love you."

"Not half as much as I love you, Nikki," he said, pulling her close and kissing her. Their kiss was cut short by a burning smell coming from the frying pan.

"I guess we'd better finish breakfast first," Nikki said, rushing to the stove.

"I'll get the table ready," Corbin offered, walking to the China cabinet. "There's a lot I need to tell you about myself, Nikki," he said, crossing the floor, carrying two plates.

"I know, Corbin, but we'll have a lifetime to catch up on our past," she reminded him.

Several hours later, Corbin Douglas and Nikki Rourke were pronounced husband and wife after a stern lecture from the judge about the P.I. forgetting to buy Nikki a wedding ring first. Corbin blushed, shrugged his shoulders, and promised the good judge the jewelry store would be his next stop.

CHAPTER *39*

As district attorney of New York and married to the lead homicide detective of the city, Bette understood better than most newly weds why her husband had to return to work ahead of schedule. A new case, the body of a woman reported missing ten days ago had surfaced and was being pulled out of the Hudson River that morning.

"The honeymoon is over," Bette whispered under her breath as she stood just inside the doorway of their home and waved goodbye to her new husband. "I didn't choose very well, did I?" she mused to herself and closed the door after his car pulled out of the driveway.

Bette returned to the kitchen and poured herself a fresh cup of coffee as she glanced at the morning headlines in the newspaper. "The lifeless body of thirty-three year old Tinker French, popular wedding coordinator at Gateau de Mers Bridal Shop, was discovered last night in a muddy embankment of the Hudson River.

"The Body will be air-lifted by helicopter this morning. Foul play is suspected.

"Ms. French is the third woman murdered in our city in less than two weeks, reports police Chief Morris Schiaffino, in an interview held late last night after the body was first discovered.

"When asked if this suspected murder could be somehow connected to the murders of Rachel Ward and Gabrielle Graves, Chief Schiaffino responded with a 'No Comment.'"

Bette sighed, laid the newspaper down, and mumbled. "Great! Just what our city needs. Another unsolved murder."

*****

Corbin Douglas noticed the silence as he and his new bride entered the

New York City Police Station. "You can almost hear a pin drop," Corbin whispered to Nikki with his arm around her waist. They continued to walk in the direction of homicide Detective Charlie Miller's office.

"Ah, here we are, darling. Charlie's office," Corbin said opening the door and stepping inside.

Charlie jumped to his feet in surprise. "Corbin!" He rushed from behind his desk.

Corbin extended his hand smiling. "Hey partner. Hope you don't mind me just popping in out of the blue like this."

Charlie shook his friend's hand, and at the same time slapped him on the back. "It's good to see you. How have you been? I've been worried sick about you."

"I have my memory back."

"Thank god," Charlie sighed in relief.

"We need to talk, Charlie."

"Sure, but I don't have a lot of time. I was on my way out. The body belonging to that young wedding coordinator…"

Corbin interrupted. "What? You mean there's been another murder? I haven't been keeping up on things. I only got my memory back yesterday."

"Sorry, amigo. Where are my manners?" Charlie said, gesturing for Corbin and Nikki to be seated.

CHAPTER **40**

Inside his mansion in Greenwich Village, Forrest Gray slumped in the chair behind his desk. "Oh, damn," he groaned. He was worried about his troubled marriage and trying to decide how he could make things right again between himself and his wife. It was crazy. Things had to change. He had hurt her, the last thing he wanted to do. Now she knew about his affairs. Well, that is, except for one indiscretion, his off and on again relationship with his wife's best friend, Sidney Cox. How he prayed she would never find out about that one.

The billionaire released another sigh as he continued to be lost in thought. 'How could I have been so stupid? Jill has been the perfect wife for twelve years. She is everything I dreamed of having in a wife. What the hell was I thinking?'

The telephone rang and interrupted the billionaire's thoughts. He answered the intrusion with a distraught, "Hello."

It was Sidney Cox. She spoke to Forrest in a soft, almost whispering, voice. "Hello, darling."

"What is it, Sidney? I'm busy." he snapped with irritation.

"I need to see you."

"I can't. Not right now. It's Jill, I'm worried about her. She's been locked inside her bedroom all morning, crying. I've hurt her, Sidney. That's the last thing I wanted to do." The billionaire's tone showed his regret.

"Jill's not as fragile as you think she is," Sidney said.

"What the hell is that supposed to mean?"

"Well, if you really want to know, Forrest, why don't you come over and I'll tell you all about that perfect little bride of yours."

"I thought you were Jill's best friend."

Sidney returned with a chuckle. "Would a best friend fuck her friend's husband behind her back every chance she got? Get real! Jill and I haven't been best friends since the eleventh grade when she stole Jason Wilkie away from me."

*****

Homicide Detective Charlie Miller and private investigator Corbin Douglas sat staring at one another, shaking their heads in total disbelief for several moments after spending the past four hours listening to the original tape recording belonging to wedding coordinator Tinker French.

The secret tapes were discovered wrapped in plastic covered by tin foil and then shoved inside a frozen TV dinner in the freezer of Ms. French's refrigerator.

"Go pick her up," Charlie finally managed, nodding his head to one of the younger homicide detectives.

"Ms. Cox, sir?" The young detective asked.

Charlie and Corbin shared a glance. "Yes, of course, I mean Ms. Cox, Turner. Get on it! Let me know when you have her in the station."

The inexperienced detective nodded and left the wedding coordinator's apartment en route to bring Sidney Cox to the police station for questioning.

"Looks like we found our shooter, eh, amigo," Charlie said, turning his attention back to his friend.

Corbin stood up. "Looks that way. At least suspicion is in play here with Ms. French's murder."

"You don't think Ms. Cox killed Ms. Ward and Ms. Graves?"

Corbin shrugged. "There still isn't any evidence linking Ms. Cox to the two murders, is there?"

"We might get lucky going through Ms. Cox's apartment."

"That's true. And of course, you could get lucky and get a confession out of her."

"There's still something we're apparently missing here. What is it?"

"The tapes give Ms. Cox a motive to murder Ms. French all right, especially with her trying to blackmail her into having sex. Ms. Cox may have been the last person to see her alive. The tapes don't reveal any confessions of murder pertaining to Ms. Graves and Ms. Ward. The only confessions on the recording were those of a very intoxicated Sidney Cox confessing the sins of her youth, experimenting in sexual discovery with numerous other young women, including her sexual activities with Mrs. Gray from time-to-time, and her secret hatred of Mrs. Gray for taking her teenage lover away from her in high school.

"Yeah, you're right, unless we get lucky and she confesses to the three murders, we're back at square one," Charlie said.

"What we need to do is figure out a motive. If Ms. Cox did kill Ms. Ward and Ms. Graves, she had to have a reason. You know as well as I do, people don't just go around whacking people for no reason." He paused. "Well, not usually anyway," he added as a second thought. "Apparently her hatred of Mrs. Gray has built up through the years but for all public appearances they seem to get along splendidly. For instance, Mrs. Gray is picking up the tab on a very expensive wedding for this supposed best friend. An obscene amount I would imagine. The wedding of the century is how the newspaper is playing it. Could it be Mrs. Gray was Ms. Cox's real target all along?"

Charlie rubbed his chin. "Maybe," he said. "Maybe Ms. Cox was having an affair with Mrs. Gray's husband too, and she wanted to cut her out of the competition."

"That or the two young dancers were trying to blackmail her. Maybe they found out Sidney Cox was having an affair with Forrest Gray too. They got jealous and tried to blackmail her," Corbin said, as he glanced at his watch.

"Well, in any case we won't be able to rule any of these scenarios out until we search Ms. Cox's apartment and, of course, talk to her. You want to come along, amigo?"

"Let me call Nikki first and see if she minds that I'm taking so long," Corbin said, walking to the telephone. "Okay if I use this one?" he asked, glancing at the detective.

"Yeah, sure. The lab boys are finished. As a matter of fact I think we can wrap it up here." Charlie motioned for everyone to wrap it up.

*****

Jill Jefferies Gray leaned across the bed and reached for her purse to get a cigarette, lit it, and inhaled several long drags. Her gaze continued to watch her young lover crossing the room to rejoin her.

"Kyle, that was amazing. I really needed it, lover," she said, patting a place beside her on the bed, inviting him to sit beside her.

"That's what you pay me for," he said, lowering his head to kiss her.

"Nonetheless, I really enjoy having sex with you. You're an amazing lover to be so young. Pity Forrest can't throw the ole' leg like you do," she said, smiling wickedly.

"If I'm so wonderful, Jill, why did you have sex with Paul Cucchiara ten days ago?" he asked.

Jill laughed and rolled her eyes suspiciously. "You've been following me again? Oh, please Kyle. Don't start that jealous bullshit with me again. I had my reasons. And as far as that goes, lover, I understand you have been fucking my so-called best friend, so I would think that pretty much makes us even, don't you think?" She pushed his hand away from her.

Kyle shrugged.

"I'd prefer you didn't have sex with my friends from now on. I pay you well enough to have exclusive rights to you. Haven't I always taken care of you, lover?"

"I have needs. And I can't always be with you when I get the urge," Kyle returned, dipping his head and kissing Jill on the nape of the neck. Chills raced up her spine.

"You are something else in bed. You always have been. Remember the first time we made love, Kyle?" She sighed at the remembered thought.

"Made love? Oh please, you seduced me." Kyle countered.

"Seduced you?"

He laughed. "I was only thirteen."

Jill ignored her lover's comment. "I'll never forget that day, lover. You were adorable. So young, so shy. I still can't get over how well-developed you were at that young age. I get wet just thinking about how delicious you were." She stretched out and put his hand on one of her large breasts.

"Oh yeah? I was something all right. When you let me stick it in you I was convinced that I had died and gone to heaven," he whispered hoarsely.

"Things were so simple back then, Kyle."

An hour later, Jill stepped out of the shower and called out to her young lover from the bathroom. "Kyle, darling, call room service and order us a nice bottle of wine. A red Bordeaux would be nice."

"Sure. How about 1945 red Bordeaux?"

"Great, lover. But make that two bottles. I don't want you to leave yet. We need to talk."

"Talk? About what?" he asked, reaching for the phone.

Jill popped her head out from around the bathroom door and smiled. "Us, darling. Is that okay with you?" she said seductively.

Kyle put the phone back down and jumped to his feet. "Don't fuck with me, Jill. The last time you told me that and didn't come across, it almost broke my goddamn heart," he said as he walked over, and pulled her into his arms.

"This time is different. This time Anthony is out of the picture." She gazed into his eyes.

"What about Paul Cucchiara?" he asked.

Jill let her towel drop to the floor as she threw her arms around her young lover's neck. "I told you, darling. I only slept with him once. I needed him to do a favor for me."

"What kind of favor?" Kyle asked, with interest.

Jill released a heavy sigh. "I had something I needed him to dispose of for me."

"Like what?"

"It doesn't matter, Kyle. What does matter to me now is us. Forrest has fucked up for the last time with me. I've had it. I want him out of the picture. Once he's out of my life permanently, then we can be together," she said, bringing his head down for a kiss.

CHAPTER 41

Homicide Detective Charlie Miller ran his fingers through his hair with aggravation, sighed, and glanced at his former partner with a frown as he stepped out of the office where Sidney Cox had been sent to take a polygraph test. "We have to let her go. Ms. Cox passed the poly. She didn't deny a thing that was on Ms. French tapes. Not a single thing or the fact that Ms. French had come to her apartment the night she disappeared."

"What are we missing, Charlie?" Corbin shook his head.

"Think we should listen to Ms. French's tapes again, amigo?"

"No. I can remember them vividly. Okay, so for the time being, let's rule out Ms. Cox since she passed the poly. Let's focus on Forrest Gray for a minute. Maybe his wife is the real target. Do you still have a tail on him?"

"Sure do. I put a couple of undercover detectives on all five of the suspects after they went strolling out of here with their high-dollar attorneys five minutes after they came in for questioning ten days ago."

"Great! So what's been going on with them?" Corbin asked.

"Well, the Grays have been putting on a front in public but have been arguing like hell behind closed doors. Mrs. Gray met with Julian's criminal attorney one night for a several hour sexathon at Trump Towers. And earlier this afternoon she had a love-in with our young bartender, Kyle Nelson," Charlie chuckled at the thought.

Corbin shook his head. "Maybe we should look a little more closely at Kyle Nelson. And Julian's attorney too."

"It's already taken care of, amigo."

"Let's go back to Forrest Gray. What's my former client been up to?"

"Well, not much. He's been going to the Scarlet Ribbon practically every night. I was told he seems depressed. He told one of the undercover agents, my brother has inside the club posing as a bartender, that he can't imagine what the hell happened to you or Nikki."

"What a pussy he turned out to be, huh?" Corbin said, shaking his head and feeling disappointed in his former client. "Here you have a good-looking, mature man worth billions. A man that has the world on a string tied around his little pinky finger and look at the dumb bastard. He's weak and indecisive; not to mention, he's a prick. Look how many lives he's ruined just by association, if nothing else."

"Yeah," Charlie said, with a nod. "Not to change the subject or anything, but speaking of guilt by association, I heard through the grapevine that Regina has been seeing Kramer Davenport again."

"Really?"

Charlie nodded. "Regina doesn't appear to be taking losing you to Nikki very well. I hear she doesn't even bother to show up for work half the time, lately. And when she does show up, she's half drunk. Pity. I tried to warn her about the company she's been keeping, but she apparently didn't listen. I also heard that Davenport beat the hell out of her a few nights ago when he was in a drunken rage."

"What?"

"Only hearsay, amigo."

"I'll break that rotten son-of-a-bitch in two with my bare hands," Corbin snapped.

"Calm down Corbin. You're a married man, remember? Let it go."

"Yeah, just the same, I'm going to pay that asshole a visit, so if you hear any 911 calls coming in at that bastard's office address, just have Dispatch ignore it." The private investigator said, reaching for his suit jacket hanging on the back of the chair where he had been sitting.

"Now wait a minute, Corbin." Charlie said, reaching out to stop his friend. "Don't go and do something you might later live to regret."

Corbin sighed. "The only thing I might live to regret, Charlie, is if I don't go over there, and kick the shit out of that mother fuc…"

"Well, if you are determined to go over there, at least watch your back. Remember who his business partner is."

"Like I'm shaking in fear," Corbin scoffed.

Charlie watched in dismay as his former partner headed for the door. "Hey, amigo," he said, stopping Corbin. "Are you coming back here or what?"

"Yeah, that is if my new bride will let me," Corbin said, giving a playful cringe.

"You want me to call your house and tell Nikki you're on your way?" Charlie offered in a last effort to change his friend's mind. And worried that he would most surely be getting ready to walk into trouble.

Determined to do what he felt he needed to do Corbin shook his head, walked out of the homicide detective's office, and closed the door.

The Shadow of Her Smile

*****

After Corbin stopped by the apartment of his former girlfriend, Regina Prescott, to check on her and to say a proper goodbye he went straight to the law office of Cucchiara, Bonfiglio, and Davenport.

It took six uniformed police officers to pull the hot-tempered P.I. off high-powered attorney, Kramer Davenport. Corbin was taken down to the police station in handcuffs, and Kramer Davenport was rushed to the nearest emergency room.

Homicide Detective Charlie Miller grinned from ear-to-ear as he watched the police officer remove the handcuffs from around his friend's wrists. He smiled and shook his head, knowing it was bound to have happened.

Charlie called out to the police officer standing outside his office, "I'll take it from here, Tyler."

Corbin dropped down into a chair.

Charlie cleared his throat. "I don't believe you, Corbin." He pretended to be angry. Unable to fulfill the pretense, he glanced at his friend, and they both began to laugh.

"Damn! I enjoyed the hell out of that," Corbin said, shaking his pounding head.

"Wish I could've been there to see it," Charlie said. "By the way, how's Regina?" he added with concern.

"Oh, shit. Don't ask. With that god-awful temper of hers, well...let's just say I was surprised she let me walk out of her apartment instead of having me carted out."

Charlie chuckled, shaking his head at the thought. He knew what a temper the female attorney did indeed have. "It went that well, huh?"

Corbin smiled. "Put it this way, Charlie. See this bruise on my forehead? Davenport didn't put it there; Regina did!"

Charlie continued to chuckle as the two men made their way down the hall to Charlie's office.

Corbin glanced at his watch. "Guess I'd better phone Nikki," he said, following Charlie inside the office.

"Some wedding day, hey, amigo?"

Corbin nodded. "You can say that again, my friend."

"You want me to have someone go and pick Nikki up and have her brought back down to the station? Or maybe ask Bette to go to your place and keep her company for awhile?" Charlie smiled mischievously and looked at his friend.

"What? Why is that grin plastered all over your face?" Corbin asked suspiciously.

"We finally got lucky." Charlie beamed.

"What do you mean partner?"

"Our young bartender phoned. He's scared shitless," Charlie said. "What's going on?"

Charlie sat down in the chair behind his desk and motioned for Corbin to sit down. "Seems Mrs. Gray asked her young stud-muffin to pop her husband."

"What?"

"Yeah, I've sent a car over to pick the poor bastard up. He should be here any time now. Maybe you should call Nikki. This could take awhile."

*****

The P.I.'s new bride was exhausted. What an amazing day it had been. She was happy to have a little time to herself to unwind and to get properly acquainted with her new surroundings. She didn't mind, in the least, when Corbin phoned and told her he wouldn't be home until late. "Wake me up when you get here," she said.

*****

After spending the next two hours listening to what Kyle Nelson had to say about Mrs. Gray, Charlie knew he had enough hearsay evidence to have the billionaire's wife brought in for questioning. With any luck, he might even have enough to arrest her for trying to get her young lover to off her husband. On the other hand, Charlie also knew that her wealthy husband's high-dollar attorneys would probably get her out of jail before the door to her holding cell had been properly closed. The police detective turned his thoughts back to his friend's comments.

"Oh, I don't know Charlie. It's all hearsay. It's Kyle's word against hers." Corbin said, shaking his head. He gave his new bride's former lover a quick once over.

Charlie nodded. "You're right. What do you suggest we do now?"

"Well we could talk to Forrest Gray. See what he has to say about his wife wanting young Kyle here to do him in. Or we could use Kyle and set a trap for her."

"Yeah, make her think her husband is dead." Charlie said, crossing the room to join the young bartender. He sat down on the corner of his desk and glanced down at him. "What do you think son? Want to help us set a trap for your sugar momma?"

"No way, man. It might backfire. And I'd hate to be on the wrong side of her if it did."

"Why did you come to us in the first place then, Kyle?" Charlie leveled his gaze on the young bartender.

"Listen Detective, you don't know Jill like I do. She can be one serious bitch if she doesn't get her way. I got scared."

"Scared?" Charlie asked. "Is that all son? Hell after what you told us about the bitch you ought to jump at the chance to get even with her. Molesting you as a young boy, using you as a play toy, and controlling your life like that? You have her to blame for keeping you mixed up and confused all these years. Making you believe she was really in love with you just to keep herself sexually satisfied. The woman used you like a whore, Kyle. How does that make you feel? It's got to end sometime. Why don't you help us now, and make yourself feel better. What do you say kid?"

Kyle cleared his throat a few moments later. "What about Mr. Gray? If he finds out I've been doing his wife all these years behind his back he will kick me and my dad out of the mansion. We'll be homeless. We have nowhere else to go. My dad will kill me if he loses his job."

"Listen Kyle, Mr. Gray is going to find out anyway. May as well come from the horse's mouth," Charlie said.

Corbin shook his head.

"I don't know Detective. Surely there must be another way. How about you question Paul Cucchiara? Jill told me that she slept with him ten days ago in order to get him to do a favor for her. When I asked her what the favor was, she just said she had something she needed him to dispose of for her. I don't know Detective Miller, but there was something almost evil about the way she said that to me. Maybe it was that gay bitch that slept with Sidney. Maybe Jill offed her. I don't know. Sidney told me earlier, that very same night, I mean the night that French broad stopped by Sidney's apartment, that after she left, she phoned Jill to tell her about French trying to blackmail her for sex. Anyway, Sidney said that after she told Jill, Jill told her not to worry about it, that nothing was going to ruin her plans for the wedding of the year. Then Jill told her that she would take care of it."

"That's all well and good, Kyle, but it isn't enough. We're back at the hearsay issue in a court of law, son. And granted, in some cases, hearsay may be enough to convict someone on similar charges, but you keep forgetting about who it is we are dealing with here. Money and tons of it. And in a courtroom, I've seen it happen time and again, money talks and bullshit walks."

Kyle shook his head. "No, I'm sorry, Detective, but I can't do it."

"Okay, let's try this on. You go home, sleep on it. Your involvement is the only way we can nail Mrs. Gray. We will be able to charge her with a murder for hire, but as far as Ms. Graves, and Ms...."

Kyle interrupted. "Hey, wait a minute, Detective. I never said anything about Jill killing those two dancers. I just told you she wanted me to do her husband, and I suggested she might have killed that gay broad, but that part was only guess work."

"Calm down, Kyle. We'll work it out."

"Can I go home now, Detective?" Kyle asked, squirming in his seat.

"In a minute. Tell me something, Kyle. In any of your conversations with Mrs. Gray can you remember if she kept any diaries, journals, or anything like that? You know, things that she may have wanted to keep hidden from her husband?"

Kyle looked thoughtful for a moment before responding. "Well I don't know about diaries, but she did ask me to find someone that would install a hidden wall safe. She wanted to put one in while her husband was out of town about six months ago. She might have something in that." He shrugged with uncertainty.

"Where did she have the safe installed?"

"In Mr. Gray's study behind some French drawing or painting she bought at Sotheby's."

"By any chance, you wouldn't know the combination to that safe would you, son?"

Corbin smiled and shook his head at how well Charlie could handle the young bartender.

"No, but I can give you the name of the guy who put the safe in for her. Would that help?"

"That's great. I want you to phone him and get the combination. Tell him not to phone Mrs. Gray. Let him know that it's a police matter. And if he gives you any shit, then I'll get on the phone. Okay?" Charlie said, gesturing to the phone sitting on his desk.

The young bartender glanced at his watch. "You mean right now?"

"Yeah, I mean right now. I know it's late but..."

The young bartender stopped the detective in mid-sentence. "Fine. I'll make the call."

Charlie crossed the room to join his former partner. Corbin smiled and shook his head. "You are a piece of work, Charlie. I can't believe you."

"Hey it worked, didn't it? Now guess what you're going to do with me, Detective." Charlie smiled and wiggled his eyebrows up and down.

CHAPTER **42**

At 4:05 a.m. four men in black ski masks, black clothing, and wearing thin latex gloves entered the private residence of billionaire Forrest Gray through a large bay window on the south side of the mansion after disengaging the sophisticated alarm system.

With graceful, catlike movements, the four experts entered the billionaire's private study. The hidden wall safe was opened and emptied of its contents within a matter of seconds. Two small cameras began clicking images of the pages of documents inside the large, white file folder, while a fingerprint expert took print samples and other traceable samples from items that might be helpful to them. A forensic specialist took one of the bullets from the gun chamber as well as other evidence that could finger the real killer of Gabrielle Graves, Rachel Ward, and possibly even Tinker French, if indeed, the gun in question turned out to be the weapon used in the deaths of these three women.

In less than twenty minutes the break-in was complete, and if all the evidence panned out, a successful mission. The four, masked intruders quickly and quietly vanished as soon as the alarm had been reset.

Thirty-five minutes later, Corbin handed two over-stuffed money envelopes to the two former F.B.I. agents and thanked them for a job well done. He turned to his friend, Charlie Miller.

"Like the good old days, eh, Charlie?" He said as he tossed his latex gloves on top of the desk inside his Manhattan office.

"Better," the homicide detective returned, as he too tossed his latex gloves on Corbin's desk. "I'll get a search warrant from Judge Malcolm first thing in the morning."

"Well, not much else we can do tonight, at least not until we get the film developed and the lab reports back from Steve and Ed. Want to talk for awhile or go home to our beautiful new brides?" Corbin asked and glanced at his ring finger. "Wearing this all the time is going to take some getting used to."

Charlie chuckled. "You can say that again. But the good news is, at least we don't have to wear the thing through our noses."

"Can you believe what has happened to us in the past ten days?"

"You've been through hell. But it seems you made one hell of a come-back, amigo."

"You mean Nikki?"

Charlie nodded. "Yeah. She's something, isn't she? A real little heart-stopper."

Corbin grinned. "I'm a lucky man, Charlie. Memory or not, it was love at first sight for me. I was doomed the moment I saw her smile."

"Well, I just hope it lasts, amigo."

"Charlie, my friend, as you well know, there are no guarantees in life, but I'm sure as hell going to give it my all. I think I'd gladly walk through the flames of hell to keep Nikki safe and with me."

Charlie chuckled. "Hell, you say?" he mused. "I bet Forrest Gray will be one pissed off S.O.B. when he finds out you stole his woman."

"Well, shit happens," Corbin returned, shrugging his shoulders.

"Losing his wife and four mistresses all in just a few weeks time. Poor bastard." Charlie shook his head.

"Well, look at the bright side, Charlie."

"Yeah, amigo. What's that?"

"He still has Jacqueline Collins."

"Like I said, Corbin, poor bastard. Oh, what the hell, it serves his ass right. Putting up with that bitch, he got off easy in my opinion."

"Meaning?"

"While I was photographing the documents that were inside the yellow envelope in Gray's study, I read two different doctors records and according to those reports both Ms. Ward and Ms. Graves were several months pregnant by the son-of-a-bitch."

"No shit? That dog."

"Maybe that's what drove Mrs. Gray over the edge."

"Maybe, but I wonder why she just didn't divorce him instead."

"I don't know, but she must have had a good reason. Maybe the prick made her sign a prenuptial agreement or something. Guys like him, I mean men with lots of cash, usually do before they take the plunge. Maybe that's why she stayed with him all these years."

"Maybe. Or something like that anyway." Corbin said, and glanced at the time again. "Well partner, let's call it a night. I have a headache the size of Stephen King's Buick 8." He closed his eyes briefly and then opened them again.

"Sure thing, amigo. Speaking of headaches, how's that hard head of yours doing since the knock on your noggin?"

"I'm not sure. But I had a pretty good nurse. Guess I better have myself checked out soon, though. I'd hate to have a relapse or something, especially after Regina hit me in the goddamn head with a lamp. Then of course, there was the two-step I did with Davenport right after Regina kicked the shit out of me."

*****

Two days later, "the wedding of the century" as it was dubbed by the press, went off beautifully. But the dinner party ended on a sour note when the groom caught his beautiful bride kicking it in the coatroom with a handsome bartender by the name of Kyle Nelson.

And when all the evidence that was taken from the hidden wall safe inside the private study of the billionaire's Greenwich mansion came back in, Jill Jefferies Gray broke down and confessed to the murders of Gabrielle Graves, Rachel Ward, and Tinker French.

When Jill was asked why she did it, she glared at the reporter who asked the question and replied, "If I had let those little tramps have my husband's babies, then I wouldn't have been his baby anymore."

Asked why she murdered the gay wedding coordinator as she was being put inside a police car, Jill glanced back over her shoulder and said, "No one, and I mean no one, was going to ruin the wedding of the century!"

*****

"Turns out," Corbin said, explaining things to his new bride, "there was a little more behind the murders of your friends, Nikki, than just Mrs. Gray being worried about not being her husband's baby anymore. Before their marriage twelve years ago, Mr. Gray had Jill sign a prenuptial agreement before he would marry her. If the marriage didn't work out, Jill would be forced to walk out of her marriage without a dime. She wouldn't have been allowed to take one single thing with her. Clothes, jewelry, nothing. So as security for herself, in the event her marriage failed, Jill dreamed up a plan where she would buy expensive things at Sotheby's Auction House and pay an unnamed source to make copies of the original items she purchased like paintings, furniture, or whatever, and then have another accomplice take the originals to a different country and re-auction them off, putting those monies into a numbered Swiss bank account, a number Mrs. Gray swears she will never reveal." He paused and then went on.

"So you see Nikki, Jill was terrified of having to leave the marriage penniless. She had Juliano put a hit out on Camellia Villano first, because of Camellia's blackmail attempt. The thought of Forrest Gray finding out that his perfect wife

Victoria Taylor Murray

was a fake from the get-go was more than she cared to deal with. That, and of course, she didn't want her husband to know that her former lover was a mobster. And after she found out her husband had managed to get two of his young mistresses pregnant, I guess she just lost it. That's when she decided to ask Kyle to take him out of the picture permanently. With Juliano behind bars he was no longer useful to her, so she thought she would use Kyle. Thank goodness, he got scared and came to the station, or this case might never have been solved."

*****

As for Clay Warner and Sidney Cox, their marriage was annulled, Sidney moved in with boyfriend, Kyle Nelson.

Forrest Gray bought himself a secluded little island paradise in Tahiti and severed all ties and connections in New York. As quoted by the press when the billionaire bid New York City a fond *adieu*, he said, "The memories of the city I once loved have become so painful, I no longer want to live here."

"And where are the homicide detective and the famous P.I. that cracked this unusual case wide-open going?" they were asked as they were preparing to board their flight.

Charlie smiled at his friend and nodded as he ushered his bride onto the plane. "You take it, *amigo*," he said.

The famous P.I. smiled and pulled his wife into his arms and whispered, "We're taking our beautiful new brides on a real honeymoon to Greece."

Additional Books from Just My Best, Inc.

Possibilities - By Janet Sue Terry

ISBN Number -0-9720344-1-2

She had definitely wanted to avoid the scene he threatened. But there had been more to it than that. A war was being waged within her. On one hand she hated Blake Baxter, and on the other, he fascinated her. And in this case, her weaker side won. PB $16.98 + $3.50 S&H

Resolutions - By Janet Sue Terry

ISBN Number -1-932586-10-5

"There are many resolutions, the trick is finding the right one." Could their marriage be saved? Or was it too late? Would Blake's hasty move to kidnap Nora and hold her captive in his ramshackle cabin in the woods backfire in his face? Or could he possibly reclaim her heart? PB $15.98 + $3.50 S&H

Angel of Death - By Rosanna Filippello

ISBN Number -1-932586-07-5

Shey had three murders and not one witness or suspect. Angelo didn't like dead ends. What did the victims have in common? They had all gotten away with crimes. They were all on probation or parole. She would have to check with the Parole Office in Spring Garden. PB $15.98 + $3.50 S&H

Angel of Justice - By Rosanna Filippello

ISBN Number -1-932586-10-5

He probably had roots in the community, but that never stopped them from fleeing the jurisdiction. Since he left no DNA evidence, he could start fresh somewhere else. They had to catch him and catch him soon. Before someone else got raped or murdered. PB $16.98 + $3.50 S&H

More On Next Page

Vacant Spaces - By Mark Andrew Ware

ISBN Number 1-932586-10-5

To discover the truth behind her friend's mysterious disappearance, Ashley Malone must uncover the evil secrets of the residents in the sinister old brownstone and unveil the truth of her own forgotten, diabolical past! PB $16.98 + $3.50 S&H

Thylacine Conspiracy - Bill Cromer

ISBN Number 0-9720344-8-X.

A suspense novel by Australian native Bill Cromer. Is the Tasmanian Tiger really extinct? If so why do sightings continue to occur? Where are the fresh thylacine skins coming from? A suspenseful trip to Tasmania, Australia and a near-death experience only piques our unlikely investigator's curiosity. PB $16.98 + S&H

Crippled Dreams - By David Rehak

ISBN Number 1-932586-12-1

Alex falls madly in love with his brother's lover, but will she return his feelings? Can she, too, overlook his crippled condition and be serious about him? PB $13.98 + $3.50 S&H

Celebrate Christmas On A Shoestring Budget
By Conni Berfield Hood

ISBN Number 1-932586-14-8

Hand-Crafted Gifts & Decorations, Activities, Recipes, Folklore Customs, Gift Suggestions. Christmas is what we each make of it; the effort one extends in creating a magical month of bliss for others and yourself. What stands out are the special events spent with family, friends, the tree trimming and decorating; the sights, sounds and smells of Christmas; the special foods and beverages reserved for the holiday season; and the enjoyment of crafting gifts. PB: $16.98 + $3.50 S&H

The Toonies Invade Silicon Valley
By Betty Dravis

ISBN Number 1-932586-29-6

Beware, citizens of Silicon Valley--the bad Toonies are on their way. Led by the evil ape-bird, Dab, the Mischief-Makers have escaped from Computer Cartoon Land. They are skulking in the shadows, ready to pounce. Dab will do anything to stay in the real world, so makes plans to take over Orange Computer, then Grape Computer, Banana ... and then the world. PB $14.95 + $3.50 S&H

http://www.jmbpub.com
Email support@justmybest.com

Or send check or money order to:
Just My Best, Inc., 1746 Dailey Road
Wilmington, Ohio 45177

Available at most online book stores and
on special order from your local brick-n-mortar
book store.

An Elite Publishing Company

Printed in the United States
32747LVS00002B/19